To Jodie

Fire in the Village

Best wishes
Ann McDunn

BOOKS BY ANNE M. DUNN

Fire in the Village: New and Selected Stories (2016)

Uncombed Hair, poetry (2005)

Winter Thunder: Retold Tales (2000)

Grandmother's Gift: Stories from the Anishinabeg (1997)

When Beaver Was Very Great: Stories to Live By (1995)

ANNE M. DUNN

FIRE IN THE VILLAGE

New and Selected Stories

Illustrations by Annette Humphrey

HOLY COW! PRESS
DULUTH, MINNESOTA
2016

Cover art and illustrations by Annette Humphrey.

Author photograph by Margaret Noel Photography.

Book and cover design by Anton Khodakovsky.

The Publisher is grateful to Beverly Slapin for her careful editorial

attention to these stories.

Printed and bound in the United States of America

First printing, 2016

ISBN 978-09864480-5-8

10 9 8 7 6 5 4 3 2 1

This project is funded in part by grant awards from the Anishinabe
Fund of the Duluth Superior Area Foundation, the Ben and Jeanne
Overman Charitable Trust, the Elmer L. and Eleanor J. Andersen
Foundation, the Cy and Paula DeCosse Fund of The Minneapolis
Foundation, the Lenfestey Family Foundation, and by gifts from
generous individual donors.

Holy Cow! Press books are distributed to the trade by Consortium
Book Sales & Distribution, c/o Ingram Publisher Services, Inc.,
210 American Drive, Jackson, TN 38301.
For inquiries, please write to: Holy Cow! Press, Post Office Box
3170, Mount Royal Station, Duluth, MN 55803.
Visit www.holycowpress.org

Dedication

THERE IS NO END to those whose names should appear on this page. I look back over many generations of storytellers who lifted their voices to speak their truths. I have lived with seven generations of my immediate family. I have seen them leave and others arrive. Some of those voices are so well remembered that I hear them when a story wants to be told. In particular I hear the eager voices of my maternal grandmother, Frances Roberts Vanoss and my mother, Maefred Vanoss Laduke Arey. These were the voices that filled my listening ears with their living tales of mystery and magic, of heroes and villains. I have carried the old stories forward to the best of my abilities and added my own urgent truths with new stories. I do this without apology or remorse. If I have done my best, what more can be required?

I especially want to thank my daughter, Annie Humphrey Utech, who provided the fine cover art and inside illustrations to enhance the stories, and whose relationship with the stories is as intimate as mine.

And my dear friend, Beverly Slapin, who sometimes sees beyond my words.

And Jim Perlman, for his continued encouragement and support.

Contents

Foreword

ALL MY LIFE I have found stories irresistible. My mother and father told stories. My maternal grandparents told stories. My great-aunties told stories. They only had to say, "Come here, my girl. I have a story that wants to be told."

This would bring me to their side where I would sit enthralled by mystery and magic. As they'd create a panoramic stage for their characters, I'd see it unfold in colorful detail.

I was a quiet child with a gift for remembering. The elders appreciated my listening heart. So I heard many stories as I was growing up. Unfortunately, I've been unable to retain all of them.

A fellow storyteller once asked, "How many stories can you tell?" About twenty-five, I said. But when she asked me to list them and count them on my fingers, I discovered that the list was easily doubled.

It's also true that some stories are told more often because they are the ones that *want* to be told. They are the ones that teach the vital lessons of our culture and traditions.

I have also read stories that found a place in my imagination, where they lived and thrived and distilled themselves into new stories that I thought were my own and so they were birthed again.

My mother always said that stories have long legs and are always ready to travel. This wisdom was brought to my attention many times during my seventy-five years. Indigenous people from all over Turtle Island would say, "That story you told is very much like a story my elders tell."

They would usually tell the part of their story that was like mine. Then they'd tell the part that was very different and we would wonder how that came to be. Well, of course, it's like Mama said, stories have long legs and sometimes they meet somewhere and exchange their truths.

My mother also said that a storyteller must respect the spirit of the story. A story must be told from beginning to end. Not begun at some convenient point and abandoned prematurely like a deserted child.

She also said a story must be carefully composed and told well. If you consented to tell a tale, she demanded that you tell it to the very best of your ability. A sloppily told story was not to be tolerated. She held herself to a high standard and there is where she held me, too.

Stories cannot simply be lifted from the page, memorized and retold. There is a certain transformation that occurs along the way. I'm dazzled by their ability to fit themselves so skillfully into my mouth, then shift from spoken to written with the graceful ease of an accomplished dancer.

There are some Indian storytellers who will tell certain stories only between first frost and first thaw. While I respect this tradition, I have come to accept the fact that there is always snow somewhere on Turtle Island, and my primary concern is in agreement with my elders. In our household stories were not reserved for winter. When is the proper time to tell a story? According to my elders, it was when a story wanted to be told.

There are private intimate stories that are told only within our home. My mother did not repeat them beyond our family circle and I continue to protect them as well. But as I watch my great-grandchildren bow their heads over computer games and their thumbs busy with digital tasks, I have come to imagine that these are the stories that will die with me.

The storyteller is usually a recognized member of the community, one who carries the stories that must be told. Perhaps young tellers will arrive to carry them forward. So our stories will continue to be passed from generation to generation.

As is expected, stories change along the way. They are expressed according to the hunter and the game, the land, the sky and the season. Most importantly, they must address the needs and concerns of those who listen. My mother said that when people hear a story three times, they are obligated to tell it. Two times is not enough. But after three times they *must* tell the story. She said, "Tell it to a stone, or a tree or a star."

I do not want these stories to be so exclusive that they die on the page. My mother said that a story is alive only when it is carried on the breath of the teller to the ears of those who hear. She said that if we do not send the stories out on our living breath they are forgotten. This is how the stories die.

I think she meant that the voice of the storyteller is a unique instrument. I can still hear her voice in the stories I tell.

Those who know me tell me that my voice changes before the story begins. That's how they know a story wants to be told. When I worked in the high school, I would see how the students relaxed and quietly looked at me when they heard me changing to my storytelling voice. This happened in the jail, too, when I was a volunteer. The inmates would sit down, stiff and full of resistance, but when the storyteller voice swept over them they became alive and alert to the story. They were a truly appreciative audience. Perhaps their captivity made them more eager for a diversion.

I believe that the voice that changes before the story begins is the voice we lose when we do not tell our stories.

To celebrate my seventy-fifth journey around the sun I have collected seventy-five stories for *Fire In The Village*. Some are gleaned from: *When Beaver Was Very Great, Winter Thunder* and *Grandmother's Gift*.

Stories that I remember are nestled up against stories I have contrived. I can't say I invented any of them because everything here has been said before. I usually begin a story with the words "I have been told" so everyone will know I am not sharing any original insight into old truth. Someone has already done that—and it may have been very long ago.

I want these stories to stand on their own feet. I want to thrust them out into their limelight and let them squirm. I send them forth as little ambassadors in search of understanding and reconciliation.

In the long ago times, a story was an oral vehicle to express cultural expectations and guide children. It also carried history and location in the details. Some of these old stories became epics, but many have been lost on the journey to this new day. Stories have made a vital contribution to the wellbeing of the people. So the substance of these new tales will be tested.

When Beaver Was Very Great

IT HAPPENED in the long, long ago that Beaver was very great. He walked upright and stood as tall as the tallest two-legged. Beaver was also highly intelligent and deeply spiritual.

Beaver had the ability to improve his environment and make it more hospitable for many other animals, too.

Beaver established communities of families who worked together to build great earthen lodges. The lodges were so well constructed that Beaver did not have to gather wood for fires to heat the lodges.

Beaver did not have to make robes or clothing of any kind because he and his family were blessed with fur-covered bodies.

Beaver had wonderful long sharp teeth that allowed them to fell large trees with ease. Beaver and his family often cut trees for their human neighbors, whom Beaver had grown to pity. In exchange, Beaver asked only for the tender bark and twigs to store for winter food.

During warm weather, Beaver probed the bottom of lakes and rivers for roots and relished many kinds of greens.

Beaver made long canals and built fine roads throughout their territory that made transport and travel easier. Beaver and his family shared the canals and roadways with their neighbors.

The two-leggeds learned many good things by observing Beaver.

Beaver bathed several times a day. Soon, two-leggeds adopted these habits of cleanliness and good grooming practices.

Beaver and his family were excellent parents and raised respectful, industrious children. So the two-leggeds imitated Beaver's parenting skills.

Beaver worked hard to accomplish good deeds that would benefit the entire community. Beaver and his family did not quarrel or fight among themselves, nor did they make enemies of their neighbors. They experienced no jealousy when others excelled.

Therefore, as time went on, Beaver prospered more than the two-leggeds.

So a delegation of two-leggeds went to Creator and reminded him that he had promised that they would be the greatest of all created beings. Then they pointed out that Beaver had surpassed the two-leggeds in many things.

The two-leggeds demanded that Creator do something to restore their original role and reduce the status and power of Beaver.

Creator said, "If the two-leggeds need an advantage over Beaver in order to surpass him, I will limit Beaver's stature and cause him to desire to live only in, on and near the water."

The delegates were satisfied and returned to their lodges.

Beaver and his family did not diminish all at once, but each generation became smaller than the one before, and after many seasons they became the beavers we know today.

But Creator allowed Beaver and his family to retain all their previous skills. They are still intelligent, industrious, and generous. They still work together to modify their habitats and build secure lodges, which they share with their extended families.

They are still affectionate, considerate, and kind. They do not fight and quarrel among themselves and have few enemies.

Beaver's greatest enemy is the two-legged, who learned so many things from our little brother, but failed to learn the important lesson of building inclusive communities.

Chipmunk

LONG AGO Creator appointed Porcupine to be the leader of all the forest animals. Soon after he took his position, he called them together for a meeting.

When they had all arrived, he stood and asked, "Shall we have night and darkness all the time, or shall we have day and sunlight all the time?"

This was an important question and much discussion followed.

After a long debate those in favor of darkness appointed Bear to explain their position.

"Night is best," Bear sang. "We shall have night. Never will the light fall upon us as we roam our dark world."

But Chipmunk, who wished for night to be followed by day, disagreed.

Chipmunk sang, "The light will come. We shall have day. But night will separate the days. We shall have day."

While Chipmunk sang, the sun began to rise, filling the forest with light. When Bear saw that Chipmunk's song had more power than his own, he became angry and tried to stop Chipmunk.

The followers of Bear were angry, too. They chased Chipmunk, who sang as he ran.

Chipmunk managed to escape into a hole just as Bear's huge claws scraped his small back, leaving the marks he still carries today.

But because of Chipmunk, day and night have followed each other through the circles of time from that day to this.

Fisher's Reward

LONG AGO, when Earth was rich with life, the water was clean, and the air was clear, all the animals were friends and spoke a common language. Because they were friends and spoke a common language, they often gathered to celebrate great and small events.

It was during such a celebration that Bear looked up into the sky and saw a strange thing.

"Look," he cried. "A dark robe is falling over the day star!"

Then all the animals looked up and saw that it was true. Soon, darkness covered the Sun and engulfed the Earth. Nothing like this had ever happened before! The animals were frightened and confused.

"Something must be done," said Bear.

So the great animals gathered at the council hill to discuss what to do.

Already the darkness was growing cold, and the tender plants had begun to wither. The small animals waited for the great ones to do something. They waited and waited, and while they waited, the great ones went on talking and talking and talking.

At last, Fisher came forward to address the council. "Let me help," he pleaded.

But Bear, who was very kind, said, "Oh, Fisher. You're too small. There's nothing you can do. Such a great problem can only be resolved by the great ones, and we are the great ones."

So Fisher went away.

Then the great ones decided that Bear should go to the top of the high council hill and see what he could do about the darkness.

So Bear climbed to the top of the hill, raised up to his full height and, growling fiercely, slashed at the darkness with his great black claws.

But it was no use. It was still dark. So Bear returned to the conference, and the great ones went on talking.

Again Fisher came forward. "Please, let me try to help," he said.

But Deer, who was very patient, said, "No, Fisher. You're too small. This is a great problem. Such a problem can only be solved by the great ones and we are the great ones."

So Fisher went away.

At last, the great ones decided that Deer should go to the top of the high council hill and see what he could do about the darkness.

So Deer climbed to the top of the hill, stood on his back legs, shook his great antlers, and ripped at the darkness with his sharp black hooves.

But it was no use. It was still dark. So Deer returned to the council meeting of the great ones, and the great ones went on talking.

For a third time Fisher came forward. "Please. Let me try," he said.

But Mountain Lion, who was not as kind as Bear or as patient as Deer, said, "Fisher, I'm tired of your silly talk. This is a serious matter we are discussing and your interruptions are not helpful. You're too small! Stop your foolish chatter and go away!"

So Fisher went away.

Then it was decided that Mountain Lion should go to the top of the high council hill and see what he could do about the darkness.

So Mountain Lion climbed to the top of the hill, leaped into the sky, snarled viciously and tore at the darkness with his mighty claws.

But it was no use. It was still dark. So Mountain Lion returned to the council meeting and the great ones went on talking.

Once more Fisher came forward. "Please, let me try. I only want to help," he begged.

Before anyone could say anything, Bear spoke. "Very well," he said. "You may try. Truly, the great ones have been unable to resolve the problem and surely you can do no harm."

So Fisher ran to the top of the hill. At the top he stopped to gather all his Fisher strength. Then he leaped up into the sky, pulling at the darkness with his small paws.

But it was no use. It changed nothing and the darkness prevailed. So Fisher leaped again and again and again. Again and again and again he fell back to the Earth. All his efforts changed nothing.

At last Bear said, "Oh, Fisher! Please stop! You're hurting yourself."

But Fisher did not seem to hear Bear.

Instead he ran to the bottom of the hill and lay down to rest. As he lay there he prayed. "Oh, Creator, help me run up this hill faster than I have ever run before. Help me leap higher than anyone has ever leaped before. Help me bring light back to Earth."

Then he ran up the hill faster than he had ever run before and leaped higher than anyone had ever leaped before. Then—he touched the darkness with his small paws and fell back to Earth.

So the darkness fell away from the face of the Day Star, and light filled the sky and covered Earth.

Such an event was surely worthy of a celebration! So the animals began to sing and dance, and the great ones made long, loud, proud speeches.

At last Porcupine stepped up and said, "We would like to hear from Fisher, for it was he who brought the light." So Bear said, "Fisher, do come forward. We want to honor you for prevailing against the darkness and restoring light to the Day Star."

But Fisher did not come forward and no one could find him.

Then Bear remembered that he hadn't seen Fisher since he'd fallen back to Earth on the high council hill. So he hurried up the hill, followed by all the other animals.

They found Fisher, but he was dead.

So they gathered around his small broken body and mourned his death.

Creator heard the sound of their grieving and came to the council hill. Gently, Creator lifted Fisher and carried him up into the sky. Creator placed Fisher in the northern part of Ishpiming, way over there, and marked the place with a star.

Then Creator returned to the council hill and told the animals this: "When you go out at night, you will see Fisher's star shining in the north. You will call it the Home Star because this is the star that will guide you home. And when you see Fisher's star shining in the north, remember: Fisher was not a great one! Indeed, he was very small. Remember this, too. Remember that although he was small, it was he who prevailed against the darkness and brought light and warmth and life back to our cold, dark dying Earth.

Our Foolish Friend

ONE FINE EVENING in the long, long ago, our friend Rabbit came out of his snug burrow and found that a gentle snow was falling. He brushed bits of leaves and twigs from his big bushy tail and, being in good spirits, began to run in a large circle. Around and around he ran. As he ran, he sang a song.

As he ran, and as he sang, more and more snow fell. Soon, he noticed that the trees were getting shorter and shorter! He believed that his song caused this to happen, so he ran on, singing as he went.

At last he became very tired. Being unable to find his burrow, he settled down in the crotch of a little willow and went to sleep. He slept for two days!

As he slept, the weather became warm and the snow melted. The snow and frost spirits had suddenly returned to the far, far north. Spring had come to Rabbit's home in the swamp.

When Rabbit awakened, he found himself sitting high up in the crotch of a tall tree. Now, our friend Rabbit had never climbed a tree—and he'd never been very brave, either. So you can imagine how surprised and frightened he was to see what had happened!

Rabbit knew that he would certainly starve if he did not get out of that willow tree. He decided he would have to jump.

Well, he gathered all his courage—and it wasn't much—closed his eyes and leaped. Just then, his nice, big bushy tail got caught in the crotch of the willow tree and broke off!

He landed on the Earth with such force that his front feet were pushed back into his body. Now they were shorter than his hind legs. He also struck his face on a sharp stone and split his lip! But worst of all, he no longer had a big bushy tail. All that was left of his fine tail was a little bit of fluff no bigger than an otter ear.

Now, every spring, the willows sprout little tufts of white fur to remind us that spring has come again—and to warn us not to be foolish like our poor little friend, Rabbit.

Tamarack and Chickadee

IT HAPPENED in the long ago that Tamarack was evergreen, like Red Pine. We Ojibwe say its beautiful, green, cone-shaped form graced the woodlands all through the winter.

But one day during a terrible storm, Chickadee was flung from his shelter and crashed into the icy snow below. He injured his small wing and found himself unable to fly to a safe place.

Within a few minutes he was nearly dead from the wind-driven cold. The little bird struggled through the blowing snow until he came to the foot of Tamarack.

"Please drop some of your lower branches to shelter me from the storm!" he cried. "I'm dying and I want to live."

"I should say not!" Tamarack quickly replied. "I did not grow beautiful green branches to break them off for you. I'm sorry but I cannot help you. I prefer to keep my fine form."

So Chickadee pulled his small battered body to the foot of Red Pine.

"Please drop some of your lower branches to shelter me from the storm," Chickadee cried. "I'm dying and I want to live."

Red Pine pitied Chickadee and quickly dropped enough branches to shelter the little bird.

Now Creator saw all that had happened and said to Red Pine, "From this day you will be self-pruning. You will always drop your lower branches to remind others that you paid a high price so a small bird could live."

When Tamarack heard this, he was glad he had not dropped any of his branches.

"Now," he thought, "I will keep my fine form."

"Yes, Tamarack," Creator said, "you will keep your fine form. But from this day, your needles will begin to turn brown and then they will fall off. Soon you will die and be forgotten."

Tamarack wept. "The punishment is too harsh!" he cried.

Chickadee had crept out from under Red Pine's branches lying in the snow. He pitied Tamarack.

"Oh, Creator," Chickadee prayed, "please don't let Tamarack die and be forgotten!"

"Very well," Creator said to Chickadee.

Then turning to Tamarack, Creator said, "You will not die and be forgotten. But every autumn, your fine green needles will turn brown and fall off. Then you will stand naked in the forest all winter, as a reminder to others that it is always better to be kind and merciful, rather than vain and selfish."

Weasel

THERE WAS A TIME in the long ago when Weasel did not change his coat in the wintertime.

But Weasel was quarrelsome, rude and unkind to other animals and Creator decided he needed a lesson.

One day Weasel, who had been quarreling with his neighbors all day, ran into a hollow log to hide from them.

But to his surprise he found he was not alone. Inside the log were several Little People.

They told Weasel that they didn't think he should be so quarrelsome, rude and unkind to others.

But Weasel only mocked them. "I will be unkind to you as well, if you don't get out of my log and leave me alone!" he yelled.

Now, the Little People are not without power and they decided to take action to keep Weasel from hurting them.

Quickly they pulled Weasel out of the log, rolled him up in a piece of birch bark and sat on him. Weasel could hear them talking about what terrible things they would do to him now that he was helpless.

Weasel was so frightened that he stuck the tip of his long tail into his mouth and began sucking on it for comfort.

After awhile the Little People left and Weasel chewed his way out of the birch bark roll. He felt just as good as he always had and thought that the Little People had not done him any harm.

But when he left the log he looked down and found that, except for the tip of his tail, he was snowy white.

At first being white didn't bother Weasel but he soon discovered that it was difficult to hunt because he could not sneak up on his prey. Nor was he able to hide from those who hunted him.

So he asked Creator to reverse the spell that the Little People had cast upon him.

Creator said, "It was not without good reason that the Little People cast the spell upon you. I cannot reverse it, but I can change it. From now on you will wear this white coat only when there is snow on the ground."

So Weasel has become a reminder to our children that we should treat others with kindness and respect.

The Promise

FOX HAD BECOME very sick from something he'd eaten and he lay down to die. He was in great pain when Mouse came along.

"Why do you lie there as one who is dying?" asked Mouse.

"Because I *am* dying," groaned Fox. "I'm too sick to reach the good greens that will cleanse this poison from my body."

Mouse said, "Tell me what to do. I will help you."

Fox told Mouse where to go and what to look for. Then Mouse scampered off.

When Mouse returned with the greens, Fox ate them and within a few minutes he was able to stand.

"Thank you, my small friend," Fox said. "I will never forget what you have done. I will tell all my relatives. We will remember forever. This is my promise."

By and by Mouse came upon Wolf, who was blind.

"Help me!" Wolf cried. "I must get to the clear water that runs in a shallow stream near the edge of the forest. Then I can wash the infection from my eyes and I will see again. Please help me."

Mouse said, "I will lead the way. Follow the sound of my voice."

So Mouse led Wolf to the shallow stream. Wolf washed his eyes and soon he could see well enough.

"Thank you, my small friend," said Wolf. "I will never forget what you have done. I will tell all my relatives. We will remember forever. This is my promise."

By and by Mouse came upon Eagle, who had a snare around his neck. Eagle was gasping for air and was unable to move.

"Help me," croaked the great bird.

Quickly Mouse chewed through the snare and set Eagle free.

When Eagle was able to breathe, he said, "Thank you, my small friend. I will never forget what you have done. I will tell all my relatives. We will remember forever. This is my promise."

So Mouse went on his way. He led a safe, happy life and raised many children. He often told his family how he'd saved Fox, Wolf and Eagle from certain death. He repeated the promise each had given him.

When Mouse was ready to cross to the other side, he told all his relatives: "Remember," he said, "we have nothing to fear. We have the promise. Fox, Wolf and Eagle have said that our relatives will always be friends."

But after Mouse crossed over, the children of Fox violated their father's promise and began to eat Mouse's children. Wolf's children also began to eat Mouse's children. Eagle's children did likewise. And so mice were hunted, killed and eaten by their former friends.

The promise was no longer spoken of and soon it was completely forgotten.

How Grasshopper Tricked a Trickster

ONE MORNING Coyote got up early and went out to hunt. Soon he found four fuzzy bunnies asleep in their warm burrow. Their mother had gone to find clover and greens.

Quickly Coyote devoured the helpless little ones.

Now Grasshopper was sitting nearby and saw everything.

When Mother Rabbit returned she was horrified to discover that Coyote had eaten all her babies. Of course, her heart was broken and she began to weep. Her pitiful cries could be heard far away.

Coyote heard the cries and knew why Mother Rabbit grieved, but he didn't feel sorry for her.

"I must eat, too," he told himself. Then he lay down to sleep under a tree.

But Grasshopper felt sorry for Mother Rabbit and went to talk to her.

"Grandmother," he said softly, "I'm appalled at Coyote's heartless conduct."

"Yes," Mother Rabbit sobbed. "He could have left at least one baby to comfort me through this time of grief."

"We will teach him a lesson," Grasshopper said. "I already have a plan."

Rabbit wanted to help. "What can I do?"

"You must make a small flute for me to play."

So Rabbit wiped away her tears and set about making a grasshopper flute. First she cut a short piece of willow with her sharp teeth, tapped the bark loose, and slipped the wood out. Then she cut four tiny finger holes in the bark. Carefully she prepared the mouthpiece, adjusted a bearberry leaf over the air hole, and presented it to Grasshopper.

"This is a very fine flute," he said. Then he took the flute and hopped up into a jackpine tree where he sat on a low branch.

Quickly Rabbit bounded off to hide in a shallow hole where she could watch what happened.

Grasshopper played a beautiful melody on the flute.

"Who is playing that wonderful music?" Coyote thought. "I must find out."

So he followed the sound to the jackpine where Grasshopper played his little flute. Coyote sat down and listened.

Then Grasshopper put the flute aside and began to sing:

> *No one plays the flute as well as I.*
> *Because I am quite small,*
> *I play the sweetest tunes.*
> *Then I sing little songs*
> *To charm the biggest beasts.*
> *I sing songs of power*
> *And my enemies are dazed.*
> *Before they know what happened*
> *I have control over them.*
> *So they walk about in confusion.*

"Ho! Little brother!" Coyote called. "That is a fine song. I want to sing that song, too. Will you teach me to sing it?"

"Of course, big brother," Grasshopper said.

So he sang the song again and Coyote listened carefully until he learned the words.

Then Coyote left. As he walked along he sang the song and suddenly he found himself sitting on a hill of fire ants. He howled and yowled and dragged his butt through the dirt until he'd shaken them all loose.

Afterwards, he tried to sing Grasshopper's song and found that he'd forgotten it completely. So he returned to the jackpine where Grasshopper sat playing his flute.

"Little brother," Coyote cried, "I've forgotten that wonderful song. Will you sing it for me again, please?"

"Certainly," Grasshopper said, and he did.

When Coyote was able to sing the song through without making any mistakes, he left.

As he went along he sang the song and suddenly he found that he'd stumbled into a deep pit. It took him quite some time to climb out of the hole. Then he discovered that the song had completely slipped out of his memory again.

So, Coyote returned to the jackpine where Grasshopper sat playing his flute. "Little brother," he called, "I've forgotten that wonderful song. Will you please sing it again?"

"Yes, I will," Grasshopper said. "But please try to remember the words this time."

"I don't know what's wrong with me," Coyote said, "I usually have no trouble remembering songs. But this time I will not forget."

So Grasshopper sang the song again and Coyote listened carefully.

When he thought the song was firmly set in his memory, he thanked Grasshopper for being so patient and went away.

As Coyote walked along, he sang Grasshopper's song. Suddenly he found himself fighting a strong current in a deep stream. He was afraid he would drown! But at last he dragged himself out of the water. Then the wet and bedraggled Coyote discovered that he'd forgotten the song again.

He hurried back to the jackpine where Grasshopper sat playing his flute.

"Grasshopper," Coyote shouted, "you must sing that song again!"

This time Grasshopper said, "What's wrong with you? I thought you were supposed to be a clever trickster. Why can't you remember a simple little song? Perhaps you aren't as clever as you say you are."

"You don't want to make me mad, Grasshopper," Coyote threatened. "Just sing that song again or I'll come up there and crush you to pieces with my great teeth."

"Very well!" Grasshopper said. Then he sang the song again.

When Coyote had the song memorized, he walked away singing. Suddenly he found himself sprawled on his back, staring up into the sky. A stone had fallen from somewhere and hit him on the head. Of course, he found that he had forgotten the song again.

As Coyote was lying on his back, Grasshopper and Mother Rabbit completed their plan by placing a stone in the jackpine. The stone had only a remote resemblance to Grasshopper. But they knew the angry Coyote would attack the stone without giving it a close look.

Then the two friends hid in the nearby hole to watch what would happen next.

"Grasshopper has enchanted me with his song," Coyote thought.

He ran back to the jackpine where he saw the stone Grasshopper sitting on a low branch.

"You tricked a trickster," yelled Coyote. "You will not be forgiven."

Then the furious Coyote leaped up and caught Grasshopper between his great teeth. But Coyote could not crush Grasshopper no matter how hard he tried, and soon all his teeth were broken off and lay in a heap on the ground in front of him.

The two friends sat in the hole and laughed until they cried.

Soon Mother Rabbit had another family of fuzzy little bunnies.

But Coyote was no longer a threat to the Rabbit Nation. So when Mother Rabbit went out in search of clover and greens she didn't worry at all about her babies. She knew they were sleeping warm and safe.

As for Coyote, he never sang Grasshopper songs anymore.

Rabbit and Otter

O NE DAY Rabbit went to visit his good friend, Otter.

"Otter," said Rabbit, "let us go camping down by the river."

"But," Otter worried, "I've never been anywhere. I might get lost! And I've never even seen the river. I can't swim. I might drown!"

"Come on," Rabbit persuaded. "I've been everywhere. You can't get lost if you follow me. You don't have to swim if you don't want to."

So Otter agreed to go with Rabbit. When they reached the river they set up their camp near the water. After they'd eaten, Rabbit said, "Let's play a game."

"No," Otter replied. "I don't play games."

"Well," Rabbit suggested, "should we dance?"

"I don't dance either," said Otter.

"Well," Rabbit wanted to know, "what do you do for fun?"

"Oh," whined Otter, "I don't have any fun."

"Of course not," snapped Rabbit, "you don't even try!"

Now Rabbit had always been a bit jealous of Otter because he had such a fine fur coat and a long beautiful tail. So he decided to have his own kind of fun—at Otter's expense.

"I'll have fun, even if he doesn't," Rabbit chuckled to himself.

"Otter," he whispered, "do you know where we are?'

"You know I don't," Otter replied.

"Well," Rabbit began, "This is called 'Where Fire Falls from the Sky.' It has been said that on cool, starry nights—like this is, when the wind sighs gently through the pines—as it's doing now, and the water flows south—as you see it is flowing at this time—it might happen on such a night that the Fire of legend will fall."

"Well," cried Otter, "I want to go home!"

"But," Rabbit quickly continued, "we're close to the river. If Fire falls, I'll warn you, then you jump into the river so you won't get any holes in your fine fur coat."

So Otter and Rabbit lay down very close to the water. When Rabbit was sure that Otter was sleeping, he took a piece of bark and, with it, scooped up the coals from the fire. He tossed them into the air and yelled—"Fire is falling!"

Otter moved like lightening and hit the water as the glowing coals came down. Then, before he knew what had happened, he was swimming!

From that day to this, Otter chooses to live close to the water. He often praises his good friend, Rabbit.

"Yes," Otter likes to say, "it was Rabbit who taught me to appreciate the pleasures of life. Didn't he take me camping? Didn't he teach me to swim? Surely no one ever had a friend as kind as he."

Rabbit is greatly annoyed by such generous praise but Otter doesn't seem to notice.

Now, Otter has far more fun than Rabbit, and when you see Otter sitting quietly on the riverbank or swimming along on his back, you will notice that he always smiles a little.

Do you suppose Otter is having a little joke at Rabbit's expense?

How Turtle
Cracked His Shell

IT HAPPENED ONE DAY in the long ago, as the aspen leaves were falling all around and the birds were preparing to fly south, that Turtle was visiting with his three best friends; Robin, Bluebird and Hummingbird.

"Why do you have to go away?" he asked. "Why can't you stay here with me?"

"Soon the Winter spirits will return to this land," Robin said.

"They bring cold and snow," said Bluebird.

"We won't be able to find food then," said Hummingbird.

"In the south it's always warm," sang Bluebird.

"With plenty of food," hummed Hummingbird.

Turtle, who was always interested in good food, said, "I want to go, too."

"Can you fly?" laughed Robin.

"Of course not," snapped Turtle.

"Well, it's a long walk," Bluebird twittered.

"Surely you can help me," begged Turtle. "If you really wanted to take me with you, you would find a way."

The birds talked it over.

Then Robin asked, "Can you hold a stick in your mouth?"

"I certainly can," boasted Turtle. "When I get something in my mouth, I never let it go."

Then Robin asked Blackbird and Crow if they would carry Turtle on a stick so he could go south with them.

"Very well," they replied.

So Turtle picked up a strong stick with his mouth. Blackbird and Crow took the ends in their talons and carried Turtle up into the sky.

Oh, it was so exciting! Turtle had never seen so many wonderful things before. He wanted to know everything. He wanted to know where they were. He wanted to know how far they had traveled. He wanted to know when they would arrive in the south.

Finally, he opened his mouth to ask one question and—he fell off the stick! He tumbled head over tail all the way down to the Earth.

When he hit the ground, his smooth polished shell cracked, but it didn't break off. He looked up and saw Blackbird and Crow still carrying the stick. But the birds were too far away to call back.

Then he felt his shell shifting in a loose and terrible manner. He suddenly lost interest in going south.

Turtle was glad to be alive, but he felt a little sick. So he found a small lake and swam to the bottom where he buried himself in the mud and went to sleep.

The following spring he awakened and crawled out of the muddy lake. He found that his shell had healed and no longer felt loose. But looking back he saw that his shattered shell had healed in a wonderful pattern. Because of this pattern, some First Nations peoples use turtle shells to mark the passage of a year.

Today, Turtle still sleeps through the winter and carries a calendar on his back.

The Lakota often point to Turtle and tell their children to learn from his example. They tell the little ones, "It is sometimes better if you keep your mouth shut!"

Thrush

LONG AGO the birds had no songs. Only First Man, Anishinabe, could sing. Every morning Aninshinabe sang to raise the sun and the birds perched nearby to listen. Every evening Anishinabe sang to set the sun and the birds listened.

The birds thought it would be wonderful if they could sing, too.

One day Creator was walking through the fields and forests of Earth. As She went along She thought how wonderful it would be if the birds could sing.

The next day She called a council of the birds. When they gathered, the shadows of their wings blotted out the light of the sun and the sound of fluttering filled the darkness.

"Do you want to sing like Anishinabe?" Creator asked.

"Yes!" the excited birds answered in unison.

"Then you must accomplish a great feat," She said. "Tomorrow we will gather here at the council rock and on my signal you will fly upward. You must fly as high as you can—to reach as close to the sky as your heart and wings will carry you. There you will find your song. Each song will be different, and you will find the sweetest song in the highest part of the sky."

Before the next sunrise, the birds were ready for the contest. Birds of every size and color gathered around the council rock.

The small brown Thrush, with bright eyes and spotted breast, considered the chances of winning the sweetest song, and slowly raised and lowered her rust-colored tail.

"I am sure that I will never be happy if I do not win the sweetest song," she said. "But how can I—with such small wings?"

Not far away sat the great Eagle, who was preening his feathers and thinking, "I am certain that I shall win the sweetest song. For who among these birds is mightier than I?"

Then Thrush got an idea. She watched the big bird carefully and when Eagle turned to clean his tail feathers, Thrush quickly hid in the breast feathers of the mighty bird.

Finally the sun rose over the horizon and at Creator's signal, the birds leaped skyward. They beat their wings rapidly against the constant pull of Earth.

Higher and higher they climbed. After some time the small birds were returning to the council rock. The low flying birds had simple songs. Some returned with one perfect note, repeating again and again.

Throughout the day many other birds returned with their songs, which they practiced to perfection.

These birds were satisfied with the songs they had won.

"It is true that we did not win the sweetest song. But we did win songs.

These are our songs! We will sing our songs the very best that we can. When we have children we will teach them to sing our songs and they will sing our songs the very best that *they* can."

So they encouraged one another and to this day you will never hear a bird sing a half-hearted song. They always sing their songs the very best that they can.

By sunset only a few birds were still flying upward. As the sun rose again, only Eagle remained in the sky.

But now his mighty wings grew heavy and beat more weakly. As Eagle was reaching his peak, Thrush flew out from her hiding place. Eagle began to pursue the small bird. But his great wings could not lift him any higher and with an angry scream, Eagle began his descent.

As Eagle came down, Thrush went up. She wasn't tired at all! She flew joyfully upward.

Then something happened that had never happened before. Thrush flew out of Earth sky and found herself in the Spirit World, where she heard the most beautiful song of all.

She stayed until she'd mastered this new music. Then she left to return to Earth. But it was a long way back and the little bird had time to think of how unfair it had been of her to cheat Eagle out of his song. She was quite ashamed! So much so, that she did not return to the council rock where the other birds waited.

Instead, she flew away to the dense woodlands of the north and hid herself in the bushes. Today Thrush still hides deep in the forest and that is why she is called Hermit Thrush.

Because she is still ashamed of how she won her song, Hermit Thrush seldom sings. But when she raises her beautiful voice to sing her flute-like song, other birds perch nearby and listen. Even we Anishinabeg stop what we are doing and turn to listen to the wonderful music that the lonely Thrush brought back from the Spirit World.

How Two-leggeds Came

IT WAS GRANDMOTHER of the Sea who brought the two-leggeds in a sack from beneath the waves. But she would need a strong helper to carry the bag across the land. So she presented it to Young Wolf who frolicked on the sandy shore.

"Carry this sack across the land," she told Young Wolf. "But do not open it until you reach the good land. I cannot tell you how terrible things will be if you open the sack prematurely."

"How will I know when I have reached the good land?" Young Wolf asked.

"You will see many lakes, an abundance of game and fish, tall birch trees, red agates and the food that grows on water."

Then Grandmother of the Sea slipped under the waves and departed.

Young Wolf carried the sack for several days. When he became tired, he stopped to rest. As he sat near the sack, he saw small movements within and became increasingly curious about its contents.

Young Wolf wondered what the two-leggeds might look like. Finally, he glanced about to see if anyone was watching, and finding himself alone, quickly opened the sack. Young Wolf was horrified to see several two-leggeds tumble out and run away!

As Young Wolf struggled to retie the sack, Old Wolf came along and helped him. Old Wolf knew what had happened, but she said nothing.

Suddenly Young Wolf, being filled with shame, went off to hide in the woods and mourn.

Wolves still gather in the woods and on moonlit hills, howling from their hiding places. They remind us of Young Wolf's remorse at having failed to deliver the two-leggeds to the good land.

So it was Old Wolf who took the sack and continued across the country. When she reached the good land, she carefully opened the heavy sack.

The two-leggeds stepped out and looked about.

They saw many animals, beautiful birds, and bright flowers. Birch trees stood all around and berries grew on low bushes. The water was full of fish and red agates gleamed in the sun. In this good land they also found the food that grows on water.

The two-leggeds were happy and thanked Old Wolf for bringing them to the good land.

Old Wolf left the two-leggeds and went into the woods, where they heard her howling with joy because she had delivered so many two-leggeds to the good land and the good life.

The two-leggeds who accidently escaped when Young Wolf opened the sack lived a very poor kind of life and were eventually forgotten.

Butterflies

I T HAPPENED in the long ago that Creator was watching some children play near the center of a small village on Turtle Island. The children were laughing and singing.

But as She watched them, Creator became sad. "These children will grow old," She thought. "Their skin will wrinkle, their joints will ache, their teeth will fall out and some will go blind. The young warriors' strength will fail! The young women will lose their graceful step."

She looked at the playful puppies yapping happily among the children. "These too will grow old," Creator thought. "The fragrant and beautiful flowers will fade. The leaves of the trees will fall."

So Creator began to pity the things that She had made.

Now, it was in the fall of the year. It was still warm and the sun was shining. But Creator knew that winter was coming, and with it, cold and hardship. Already the wind was carrying yellow leaves to the ground and swirling them about the children's feet.

Creator saw the sun casting shadows of dancing children upon the Earth. She saw the bright colors of the flowers. She saw the gold of autumn leaves. She saw the blue of the sky.

Suddenly Creator smiled. "I will make something new. I will make something that will gladden my own heart. I will make something that will delight the children. I will make something that the old ones will also enjoy."

So Creator took a spot of golden sunshine, a handful of the blue sky, the green of pine, the white of corn, the black of an infant's hair, the shades of changing leaves, the beauty of flowers, and the glory of sunrise.

To all of this She added a song.

She put the new creation in a bag and took it to the children. "Children," Creator said, "this is for you!"

She opened the bag and hundreds of colorful butterflies flew out. They fluttered around the children and settled on their hair. Then the butterflies left the children to sip the nectar from nearby flowers. Later, they gathered in the pine trees to sing.

The children were amazed! They had never seen such a wonder! Creator was satisfied.

But the birds were not pleased. For they had been allowed to sing only after a great competition. They had won their songs by flying as high as they could. Therefore, they felt it was unfair for Creator to give songs to the butterflies who had done nothing to deserve them.

Creator considered the birds' complaint and agreed. It wasn't fair to give the butterflies a song, when the birds had had to compete for theirs.

So Creator took the songs from the butterflies and that is why they are silent today. Still, they are beautiful and still they gladden Creator's heart and still they are a delight to the children and the old ones enjoy them, too.

The Birth of Wanabozho

WHEN THE GREAT FLOOD destroyed the world of the Anishinabeg, Creator took pity on the people and sent a teacher to help them make their way in the new world.

Now the birth of the teacher came about in this way.

A wise elder woman named Nokomis fell in love with a handsome stranger. Many of her friends tried to discourage her from marrying him. They told her that such a relationship at her time in life would jeopardize her status among the people.

Nokomis decided to risk her place in the community, and the man took her to the moon where they arrived young and strong. They lived there for quite some time and they were happy together.

But another woman decided that she wanted the man for herself and began planning how to get rid of his wife.

One day she saw Nokomis sitting alone on the edge of a crater lake. Quickly she ran up behind her and pushed her into the deep water.

So Nokomis fell all the way back to Earth. When she returned, she was the same as the day she had gone to the moon with her husband. Of course, she was lonely.

Then, to her delight, she discovered that she was pregnant!

Soon she gave birth to a daughter and named her Wenona.

The gentle girl grew tall and kind. Many young men wanted her, but Nokomis would not allow any of them to marry her.

Then it happened that the West Wind saw Wenona bathing in the lake with some other young women and he fell in love with her. When he went back to his wind kingdom in the mountains, he could not forget her.

So he returned one night and carried Wenona to the mountains where he kept her in his lodge with his sons North, South, and East Winds.

But Wenona escaped the mountains and found her way back to her grieving mother. Nokomis was happy again!

Not long after her return, Wenona gave birth to twin boys. Totally exhausted from the difficult labor of twin births, the gentle young woman departed to the Land of the Spirits, taking one of the infants with her.

Of course, Nookomis felt great sorrow at the loss of her daughter and grandson.

She named the living infant Wanabozho, wrapped him in soft grass and placed him under a large wooden bowl to protect him from danger or accident. She took him out only to feed and clean him. Then she wrapped him in fresh grass and put him back under the bowl.

One day she heard a rustling, and lifted the bowl to find that the infant had transformed himself into a small rabbit! He had eaten the grass that she'd wrapped him in and was looking for more.

She picked him up and held him close for the first time. She was sorry that she'd left him alone under the bowl while she grieved.

Suddenly the rabbit changed into a boy, who wrapped his arms around her neck and kissed her on the cheek. Then they wept together for those who had departed.

Nookomis loved the boy greatly and the child rarely left her side.

But as he grew tall and strong, he began to wander from her side more and more. He went into the forest where he learned many things about the plants, insects, birds, and other beings who lived on Turtle Island.

Because Wanabozho was both human and spirit, he could change himself into many things, but mostly he took the form of a young, strong, brave man.

But he also had a great sense of humor and often did things just to make the people laugh.

He was a great help to the Anishinabeg.

He showed us how to hunt and fish, where to find roots and plants for food and medicine.

He also taught the children how to get along with all their relatives. He did this through stories, songs and deeds.

So it was that he became the mythical hero of the Woodland peoples.

So it is that we are still telling of his deeds today.

Wanabozho and the Red-eyed Ducks

IT HAPPENED in the long ago—during that time when the animal people and the two-leggeds spoke the same language—that Wanabozho
went out to hunt. He was thinking of the long winter, when Cold Maker
would bring snow and ice and bone-chilling winds. He thought of how
difficult it would be to leave the warmth of his fire to go out looking for
game.

Wanabozho thought, "If I could kill many ducks, I would smoke them for
the winter. Then I wouldn't have to go out hunting when it gets cold."

So he took his small bow and his little duck arrows and went to a round
lake. He could see the whole lake from one place. There were many ducks on
the lake, many nice fat ducks. But when they saw him, they swam to the other
side of the lake and were well beyond the range of his duck arrows.

However, Wanabozho was clever and had a good idea. So he thought,
"Perhaps I will have plenty of game after all."

He went into a nearby field and began cutting the tall grass with his sharp
knife. He tied the grass into bundles and carried them to the lake so the ducks

could see him. Then he chopped the grass into small pieces, mixed it with mud and began to build a round house.

After some time the ducks became so curious that they swam close to Wanabozho and asked what he was doing.

"I'm building a round house."

"Well," one of the ducks laughed, "it's an odd house that has no door."

"It will have a door," Wanabozho replied. "Up near the top, I will make a round door. When I'm finished, I'll sit in the house and sing."

The ducks wondered what kind of songs Wanabozho would sing in such an unusual house. They all said, "We want to hear the songs, too."

But Wanabozho said, "No! I cannot sing these songs for you because they are very bad songs."

"Are you sure?" The ducks asked.

"Oh, yes," Wanabozho said. "They are especially bad for ducks."

Then the ducks became even more curious. "Sing them for us," they begged. "We'll tell you if they are bad."

"No!" Wanabozho said. "I know they are bad and I cannot sing them for you. I must build the round house and sing them as I sit alone. Truly, I cannot sing them for you," he said sadly.

The ducks decided that they would help Wanabozho build the round house. They began chopping grass with their sharp bills, and mixing and packing mud with their webbed feet. Soon the round house stood complete.

"Well," the ducks declared, "we have helped you build the round house. So we have decided that you must allow us to sit in the house with you when you sing."

"Oh, no!" Wanabozho cried. "I can't allow you to hear these bad songs!"

But the ducks insisted. "Without our help, you could not have completed the house. We have earned the right to enter with you."

At last Wanabozho agreed.

So he climbed in through the high round door and the ducks followed.

"Now, sing," they demanded.

"Oh," Wanabozho wept, "I'm so ashamed of the bad songs! Please don't look at me while I sing. You must close your eyes while I am singing or your eyes will turn red!"

So the ducks gathered close around Wanabozho and closed their eyes.

Wanabozho began to sing, and the songs were very bad.

As he sang, he reached out and grabbed a duck. Quickly he twisted the duck's neck and tossed the dead creature out the round door. Then he grabbed another one.

After he'd killed several, one wary duck opened an eye and saw what was happening.

"Wanabozho is killing us!" he screamed.

All the ducks opened their eyes and flew at Wanabozho. They beat him with their wings, nipped him with their bills and tore him with their toenails.

Wanabozho scrambled through the small door and ran away.

The ducks looked at each other through their red eyes. Then they dragged their dead companions into the house and sealed the door.

The round house has disappeared now but the ducks who listened to the bad songs have not forgotten their foolishness because wood ducks still have red eyes.

That's the way it was. That's the way it is.

Hunter's Rest

A CERTAIN MAN went out in the fall to hunt a bear. It was very cold and had begun to snow. The hunter found a bear in a hole, killed it, dragged it out and skinned it, too.

In the meantime, the cold wind had chilled the man through. So he decided to crawl into the hole with the hide to keep warm. He pulled leaves and grass over the opening of the hole and went to sleep.

When he awoke, he pushed the dried debris away and looked out. What he saw surprised him greatly. Outside of the hole lay the rotting carcass of a bear. It was covered with flies.

The man crawled out of the hole and found that it was spring.

He had slept all winter in the bear's den!

That is why the elders always say, "Never fall asleep in a bear's den."

They also say it is our good brother Bear who sends the winter spirits of snow and cold back to the far north and invites the green spirits back to our land.

Because the young hunter did not properly care for the bear he'd killed, he never killed another bear. Sometimes when he was out hunting rabbits, a bear would come along and swat him across the head! It was not a killing blow, just enough to express the contempt the bear nation had for that man.

Lost Child

IT HAPPENED in the long ago that a little girl went out to pick blueberries with her mother.

They came upon a small patch of the bright fruit and the eager child cried, "Berries! Here are berries! Let's pick them!"

But her mother said, "We must find more berries. This is such a small patch we should leave it for the bears. We'll go on farther."

They came to another small berry patch and the child said, "I want to pick these berries." So she sat down and began to pick.

"Very well," her mother said. "You pick here and I'll go on a little farther. You stay right here and wait for me. I'll come back for you." Then she left.

The little girl picked all the berries and then sat down to wait. Soon it was dark, so she went to sleep.

In the morning, she ate her berries as she waited for her mother to return. It grew dark again. The child became frightened and began to cry.

"Mama!" she cried. But there was no answer. So she cried herself to sleep.

The next day she left the place and began to walk. In a short time she realized she was lost. She sat down and cried again.

Suddenly she heard a woman call, "What's wrong, Little One? Why do you weep?"

She looked up to see a tall, handsome woman and two children coming toward her. She ran into the woman's outstretched arms. They sat down together and the woman held the child as the youngster told how she'd become lost.

The tall woman listened to the child's story and comforted her. Then she carried the young one to a nearby lake, bathed her and afterwards gathered some sweet berries and good roots for the child to eat.

"Come, Little One," the woman said. "I'll take you to your people."

How happy the child was to hear that the woman knew where her people were. She wasn't lost anymore. She was going home!

Along the way, the other two children wanted to play, but the woman scolded them. "Little One doesn't want to play. She is feeling sad. Don't bother her."

The woman held the little girl's hand as they all walked along together.

When they got close to the village, the woman pointed out the direction the girl should go. Then she took her two children and went on her way.

"Good-bye," the girl called. The woman waved farewell.

The people in the village greeted the child with great joy, for she'd been missing for several days. Her mother, however, never returned.

When they asked the child how she'd found her way back, she told them about the tall woman and led them to the place where they had parted.

The people were amazed to find the tracks of a large bear and two cubs.

Wanabozho Brings Fire

THERE WAS A TIME in the long, long ago when the Anishinabeg had no fire to keep them warm or cook their food.

In fact, they feared fire because they had seen what it could do to the forest when lightening struck.

But when Wanabozho saw the effect of the cold on his kind grandmother, his Nokomis, he decided she needed fire to warm her bones. He told her he was going to steal some fire for her so she wouldn't be cold anymore.

Now an old warrior magician who lived in the underworld with his two strong daughters guarded and protected the fire. The people had been told that the magician was vicious and powerful.

So Nokomis was frightened for her grandson.

"No!" she said. "That old magician will hurt you."

But Wanabozho was both brave and determined. Once he made up his mind to do something, he would do it.

So in the Moon of Wild Rice, he started out for the place where fire was kept. When he got close, he hid his canoe in the trees by the river.

Then he changed himself into a little rabbit and jumped into the water to get wet. He wanted to look pitiful so the old man's daughters would feel sorry for him.

The women were hanging their fishing nets when one of them saw the wet rabbit. Feeling sorry for the little creature, she picked him up and carried him inside where her father was sleeping. She placed him near the fire to dry and get warm. Then she went back to help her sister with their work.

Wanabozho hopped closer to the fire and his steps woke up the old man. But when he saw that it was just a rabbit, he went back to sleep.

When the old magician started snoring, Wanabozho changed himself into a man, grabbed a stick of fire and ran from the lodge!

The magician woke up with an angry yell.

"Bring back my fire!" he roared.

Then he sent his daughters after Wanabozho, who was running as fast as he could toward the river.

But, looking back, he saw that the women were gaining on him.

"Give our fire back to us!" they called.

Just as Wanabozho reached the canoe he looked back again and saw a large meadow of dried grass.

"Here's your fire!" he cried as he plunged the burning stick into the dry grass. Instantly the grass was ablaze and the wind carried the flames and smoke back toward the women. So they were forced to give up the chase.

Wanabozho pushed his canoe down into the water and began paddling toward his village. He was thinking about Nokomis and how warm she would be now.

As he looked back to watch the fire, he noticed how it was reflected in the leaves of the trees. He saw how they shone with brilliant colors of red, yellow, gold and brown.

It was so beautiful that he asked Creator to make the leaves look that way every fall. And that's what happened.

When Wanabozho returned to his village with the gift of fire, he found that Nokomis had dug a shallow pit in the floor of their wigwam. She'd already lined the pit with round stones from the river, laid a bed of torn birchbark and built a little tipi of dry sticks. She had more wood waiting nearby.

She was sitting alone in the wigwam when Wanabozho came.

He touched the stick of fire to the birchbark and they watched it ignite.

Then he waited for the sticks to burn. Afterwards he laid the heavier wood in the fire and sat down with his grandmother.

Although she was pleased that her grandson had done this thing, she told him,

"You took a terrible risk."

Wanabozho thought for a moment. Then he said, "I don't believe the magician had any real power, or he would have used it against me."

Then after further consideration, Nokomis replied, "It's possible that Creator allowed you to overcome the magician's power so an old woman could sit by the fire and warm her bones."

Perhaps they were both right.

Frog Vengeance

AN ELDER MAN had two sons, and each son had a son. The elder was proud of his sons and he loved his grandsons very much.

One day the three men were going out to hunt and the boys wanted to go, too. The men were pleased to see their children taking such an interest in providing food for the family, so they allowed the boys to accompany the hunting party.

The party went some distance from the village and made camp. Then they went out to see what they could find. But the boys grumbled and complained. They said they had already walked so far that they were too tired to hunt. Their loud whining frightened the game away.

So after a short while, the fathers took the boys back to camp. The elder returned later with a few partridges, which he cleaned and cooked.

Once again, the boys complained. They said they didn't like partridge meat. They said it was too dry.

But Grandfather told them, "We must learn to be thankful for what we have and express gratitude to Creator for feeding us again."

Then they sat around the fire while Grandfather told a story of how the Frog People took vengeance against those who were unkind to small, helpless creatures. Then one by one they rolled up in their blankets and went to sleep.

In the morning it was decided that the men would go hunting and the boys would remain in camp. Their fathers wanted them to rest and play.

"But you must keep the fire going," Grandfather said. "That will be your responsibility."

So the men left and the boys began gathering wood. Soon they had a large pile. While looking for more wood, they discovered that there were many frogs in the area. So they caught a few.

They carried them to camp, tossed them into the fire and watched their desperate struggle to escape the flames. The boys found torturing and killing frogs an amusing way to pass the day.

When Grandfather saw what had happened, he was appalled.

"You have done a terrible thing!" he cried. "You killed these small creatures for no other reason than that you found pleasure in their misery and death. These helpless creatures died in torment and terror. You had no pity for them! Neither shall you find pity when torment and terror falls upon you."

"Come, come," one of the men said. "Don't let yourself be so upset over a few dead frogs."

The other one said, "You're being unreasonable toward these boys. Don't forget, they are still children."

So they excused their sons for what they had done to the little frog people.

But Grandfather insisted, "A terrible act has been committed against these defenseless ones and a terrible thing will be done to you."

The men were disgusted with the old man.

One of them said, "I've lost interest in hunting."

"Yes," said the other. "I think we should go home."

So Grandfather, his sons and grandsons broke camp and began walking toward the village.

But on their way, they came to a great bog which none of them remembered crossing before.

One of the men said, "We will walk across here."

But Grandfather was troubled by the unusual way the bog had suddenly appeared. "It's not safe to cross this strange bog," he told them. "We should go around."

"No," the boys whined. "We're too tired to go around! We want to cross here!"

Grandfather did not want to argue with them, so he said, "You may do what seems best to you. I will go around."

So he left them there.

When he got to the village he was surprised to find that they had not yet arrived.

Immediately he went back to find them, but they had completely disappeared and they were never seen again.

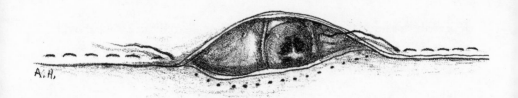

A. H.

Kills His Enemy

IT HAPPENED one day that a small boy was left at home with his blind grandfather, while the rest of the family went to a nearby village to visit their other relatives.

Now although the grandfather was blind he could see quite well with his hands. So he told the little boy, "I will make you a bow and one arrow. Then you can practice how you will protect your people from attack and prevent our enemies from stealing our fine ponies."

Naturally the child was delighted. So Grandfather took the boy a short distance into the forest and cut some strong straight sticks. Then he prepared the rawhide string and found an arrowhead that he'd been saving for just such a day. The elder fashioned the bow and an arrow while the boy watched. Because Grandfather was blind he worked slowly but eventually he had a perfect bow and arrow.

One evening they sat at their fire inside the lodge talking quietly and eating their small meal of smoked sucker and boiled cattail roots. Grandfather said, "Practice aiming the arrow at things in the lodge. Pull the bow but don't shoot anything."

So the boy would find something, aim at it and pull the string. But he didn't release the arrow. He did this repeatedly. Then he saw a small hole in the wall of the lodge and something glittering in the hole. He knew that someone was looking in on them so he continued aiming at things around the lodge until he was aiming at the hole. Then he pulled the bow and shot the arrow that went right to its mark.

A loud moan and heavy thud was heard beyond the wall.

Grandfather was surprised. "What was that?"

"I have killed an enemy," the boy said.

The boy took a torch and they went out together. There they found a dead man with an arrow through his eye.

Grandfather touched the man and said, "Yes, you have killed an enemy. It is a good thing they left me with such a brave boy. This man was trying to see if we were alone. He probably thought he had nothing to fear from an old blind man and a little boy. So he was going to kill us and steal our horses."

Then Grandfather pulled the arrow from the dead man and took it inside the lodge. He carefully carved a small face on the shaft. He carved a closed eye to indicate that the child had killed an enemy by shooting him in the eye.

When the family returned, they disposed of the body and prepared a feast to celebrate the courage of the boy and his new name. From that day he was called Kills His Enemy.

Wanabozho and Ten Greedy Men

TEN MEN from a certain village took gifts and went to talk with Wanabozho about the welfare of their people.

When they arrived at his lodge, Wanabozho called from inside, "Well, Uncles, come in if you want to see me. Don't stand around outside shuffling your feet and rolling your eyes."

So the men entered the lodge. Wanabozho shook hands with them and invited them to sit down. Then there followed a long silence.

Finally a piece of wood near the door said to Wanabozho, "Why don't you speak to your Uncles? When I was a tree I spoke with my relatives."

Wanabozho replied, "I'm just thinking about the kind of customs they may have where they come from. I was asking myself how to greet them and make them feel at home."

Then after a brief silence, Wanabozho said, "You've been walking a long time. You must be hungry."

Now Wanabozho always had all the food he needed and he kept it in a large leather sack. Inside the sack were the bones of various animals.

When he reached into the sack to find something to feed his guests, he pulled out a bear's foreleg. He threw it down before the men and it became a black bear.

The bear smiled at the men and said, "Greetings, my brothers. I understand that you have been traveling a long time. I know you are hungry and I offer myself to you."

Then Wanabozho told the men to kill the bear and cook it in the big kettle they would find at their camp. So they killed the bear, dragged it to their camp and cooked enough for one meal. Then they prepared another meal and took it back to Wanabozho's lodge. They carried the kettle on a long pole and put it down in front of him.

Wanabozho's daughter lived nearby in another lodge. He'd told her to bring birch bark dishes and clamshell spoons for their visitors. When she came she wore a red sash around her waist and large copper rings hung from her ears.

After the feast, the men returned to their own camp. But the next day they went back to Wanabozho's lodge and presented the gifts they had brought.

One man said, "I have come to ask for a life that never ends."

Quickly Wanabozho grabbed the man and flung him into the corner of his lodge. When the man struck the wall he tumbled backwards and turned into a stone.

Wanabozho said, "You have asked for a long life. Now you will last as long as the Earth."

"I want unfailing success and cunning," the next man said. "So that I may never lack the things I need."

Wanabozho grabbed the man and threw him out of the lodge.

When the others looked outside they saw a fox standing there.

"Now," said Wanabozho, "You will always be successful and cunning."

Because of what they had seen, the remaining men became frightened. They decided to ask for one thing together. So they asked that they might have healing power in their medicine.

Wanabozho put some medicine in little leather bags and gave one to each man.

"Ten men came to see me," he said. "Eight will return to their homes. The other men were selfish and asked for too much. That's why they failed. But you have asked for very little and you now have the opportunity to help your people. Use the medicine sparingly."

Then he shook hands with each one of the men.

"The medicine I give you will not last forever," he warned them.

"My daughter is the only one who can help you keep the power of this medicine. Unlike myself, she is entirely human and I want her to go home with you.

"Protect her until you get home. She will marry one of you. But do not discuss this with her until you return to your village. If you do not wait, your medicine will lose its power."

So the men started home with the woman. She sat in the middle of their large canoe as they paddled across the lake.

When they reached the shore they made camp. The woman cooked for the men, but made her own camp some distance from theirs.

It happened that they made camp four times on the journey.

All went well until the last night when the men began talking among themselves about who would be her husband.

One said, "I think she should have something to say about that. She must know whom she wants. I'll go talk to her."

The other men watched as he walked toward the woman's camp.

When the man arrived at the woman's camp, he asked her which one of the eight men she wanted for her husband. She said nothing. So after a few minutes of silence, the man returned to the men's camp.

Then another man said he would talk to the woman and he went to her camp. He found her red sash tied to a tree near her campfire but she was gone.

Because they failed to honor their agreement with Wanabozho, the medicine lost its power.

Of course, the men were unhappy. But the most miserable was the one who found her copper earrings in the bottom of his pack when he got back to his own lodge the next day.

Heart Berries

IT HAPPENED that a man and woman loved one another and wanted to
be together forever.

At first all went well. Then the man grew discontent with the woman. He
became critical and unreasonable.

"I don't like the way you cook," he complained. "I don't like the way you
laugh, and you talk too much."

Of course, she didn't like being treated with contempt, so she decided to
leave.

"I'm returning to my mother's lodge," she told him one day.

"Good!" he shouted.

So she packed her basket and left.

He didn't say good-bye and she never looked back.

During the first day of her absence the man was angry.

"She left me," he thought. "Walked right out! Took all her stuff, too. Well,
I don't care. I'm better off without her."

On the second day he felt sorry for himself.

"Now what will I do? I'm alone. I don't have a cook. No one to mend my
clothes. No one to keep me warm."

On the third day he was sorry.

"What have I done? I forced her out. I was critical, unreasonable and unkind. I deserve to be alone. But I'm sorry for the way I treated her. I want to be forgiven. I'll go after her. I'll beg her to come back. But she's been walking for three days. I won't be able to catch her before she reaches her mother's lodge. If she gets to her family they will convince her not to come back with me. I have to catch up with her soon!"

So the man packed a bag of food and started walking in the direction his wife had gone.

Creator had heard the man crying pitifully and looked into his heart. Creator saw that the man was truly sorry. He had changed his mind completely and loved the woman more than ever.

So Creator caused a great field of flowers to grow up before the woman. Many of the flowers had never been seen on Turtle Island. The woman was amazed at their beauty and stopped to admire them. She smelled their sweetness and gathered enough to braid into her hair. Then she picked up her basket and went on.

The flowers did not stop her, but they slowed her down. Her husband had gained some distance.

Then Creator caused a great forest to grow up in her way. The trees were so close together that she passed through this forest with great difficulty and it took several sleeps to reach the end.

The trees did not stop her, but they slowed her down. Her husband gained even more distance.

Then Creator caused a great field of low-growing plants to grow up around the woman as she rested. The plants were hung with bright red berries that sparkled in the sunlight.

She picked one and ate it.

"This is the most delicious berry I've ever eaten," the woman decided. "I'll fill my basket and take these berries home to my mother."

So she dumped all her possessions out of her basket and began picking the tiny berries.

As she picked the berries she ate some, too. The sweet taste of the berries made her think: "I miss my husband. I love him as much as I ever did.

I should forgive him."

It took a very long time to fill her basket with such tiny berries. So when the man came over the hill and saw her sitting among the berries, he ran to her and begged her forgiveness.

Of course, she had some doubts about his sincerity, but he promised that he would never speak to her again in an unkind manner and would always treat her with love and respect.

Creator gave her a nudge, too.

"Yes," she said, "I forgive you."

Then the man looked at her red stained fingers. "You're hurt," he cried, pressing his lips into the palms of her hands.

"No, no," she said. "It's the juice from these wonderful little berries."

Then she put one in his mouth.

He put one in her mouth.

She put another one in his mouth. He put another one in her mouth.

Then the two returned home.

She called the little fruit "heart berries" because they stopped her in the field and changed her heart toward her husband.

So they were together for many years and when he went to the other side, she was lonely again.

But she picked berries with her grandchildren every summer and as they sat in the fields picking heart berries, she told them about the long ago time.

"These are the berries that made us sweethearts again," she would say, and it made the children glad.

Some people call these sweet red fruits "strawberries," and we remember how they can mend our relationships and heal our hearts.

Old Woman and the Bear

T HERE WAS an elder woman who lived alone in a village near Leech Lake. She had no family so the community took care of her. Because she suffered from dizziness over moving water she was unable to set nets or gather rice. But she always picked lots of berries and shared them with others. Since she was a kind and generous person, her neighbors were always glad to help her in any way they could.

One day in early spring a woman came to the elder with a nearly dead bear cub.

"My children found this little one in the river," she said. "He must have fallen in and couldn't get back to his mother. I thought you could help him."

Quickly the elder woman carried the cub into her lodge. He was cold and wet. He was hungry and frightened. The woman laid a few more sticks in the fire pit. Then she sat down and cradled the cub in her arms. He looked up at her with large, brown, unblinking eyes.

"Yes, little one," she whispered. "Now you have a friend."

From the first day he seemed to know that he could trust her. He touched her cheek with his small black nose. He smelled her fragrant hair.

She held him until he was warm and dry. Then she gave him a maple sugar cake and soon he was sleeping. So she put him in her bed and covered him with a moose hide.

It was still light so she decided to make a pair of leather mittens to cover the cub's long, sharp claws. She carried a mat outside and sat down in a sunny place to cut and sew.

When she finished her work, she returned to the lodge and sat down beside the sleeping cub. She smiled at his quiet contentment. Then with gentle hands she put the mittens over his long claws and tied them in place with soft leather thongs.

She rubbed his little ears and wondered what he would like to eat in the morning. After a few minutes she got up and poured a measure of rice into a birch bark basket and added enough water to cover the grains. Then she went to bed, too. The cub didn't wake up, but he snuggled close to her all night.

In the morning they ate boiled whitefish and rice soup. After they had eaten, she made him a leather ball and stuffed it with grass. He played with that ball all day.

The woman laughed at the silly little bear and he laughed, too.

Now the woman was no longer lonely and she had someone to care for. Soon she loved the bear as she would have loved her own child.

Her neighbors brought extra food to feed the bear. So he grew healthy and strong. He played all day. In the evening he listened to the woman tell stories and sing the old songs. He seemed to understand everything she said.

The children were not afraid of the cub and would come to the lodge to ask if Little Bear could go out and play with them.

The woman always made Little Bear wear the mittens when he played with the children.

"Remember," she told him, "the children are quite tender and easily injured. I don't want you to hurt them with your claws. So you must be very careful."

Sometimes Little Bear played so roughly that he broke the children's toys. But he never hurt the children because he always wore the mittens and he was very careful.

By the end of summer he had grown quite large. The woman knew that it would soon be time for the bear to hibernate. Because he didn't know how to prepare for the long sleep, she would be his teacher.

She led him some distance from the village. As she went along she was looking for a sheltered area where Little Bear would be safe and warm and dry all winter long.

"Aha!" she shouted. "There it is."

As Little Bear watched, the woman climbed down into a large hole that had been left when a tall cedar tree had toppled. The hole was dry and the great roots formed a natural cage that would protect Little Bear from intruders.

Quickly she began filling the hole with leaves and grass. Soon she had prepared a cozy nest for her little friend.

Then they went home to wait for the first snowfall.

One day she woke up to a snow covered world. She saw that Little Bear was growing tired and drowsy. He had no interest in playing or eating. So they went back to the cedar root nest and Little Bear crawled inside. She showed him how to pull the leaves around him and then he lay down. Almost instantly he was sleeping.

She sat beside him for a long time. Then she laid a few sticks over the nest, covered it with more leaves and grass and went home.

One day in the spring she heard Little Bear come bawling through the village. To the lodge he came and fell into her embrace.

They laughed and cried and danced and sang.

Bear was no longer a cub but he was not yet full grown. Sometimes he played with the children and sometimes he went hunting with the men.

When she sent Bear out to hunt she told him, "You must be very careful not to get hurt. Stay with the men and don't get lost. I don't want to lose you. You are like my own son now."

The hunters usually returned home with much game.

"Bear is a wonderful hunter!" they said.

But one day something terrible happened.

They said a man from anther village had attacked Bear. The man said he didn't know the bear was tame.

So the woman cut strips of white rabbit skin and wove a wide collar for Bear.

"Now when other people see you," she said, "they will know that you are not a wild bear."

So Bear went hunting with the men and was never mistaken for a wild bear again.

However, in a nearby village there lived a man who was jealous of Bear and determined to kill him.

The woman had told Bear to treat all people with respect and not to harm anyone.

"But if you are attacked," she said, "you must defend yourself!"

Several days later Bear returned to the lodge with the body of the man who had vowed to kill him.

"No," the woman said, "I cannot help this man for he is dead."

The hunters were quick to defend Bear. They had seen everything. They told her the man had repeatedly attacked Bear. Bear would turn away and run from the man. But the man would chase him. He would not leave Bear alone. At last Bear had turned and struck the man so hard he broke his neck.

Bear was sorry and ashamed of what he had done but no one in the village blamed him for it.

Then one day the hunters came to warn the woman.

"The dead man has three sons," the hunters said. "They have vowed to avenge their father's death by killing Bear."

The woman was sick with grief and fear.

"You must go away, my son," she told Bear as she removed the collar. "If you stay far away, you will be safe."

Bear didn't want to leave and, weeping loudly and pitifully, he fell down before the woman. She wept, too. Although Bear was now quite large, he was as frightened as the little cub the children had pulled out of the river on that first day. So the woman held him in her arms like she had done when he was small. She rubbed his ears and sang an old song.

At last Bear went way and she never saw him again.

But sometimes when hunting had been poor and the men came home without game they would find a moose hanging in the tree near the woman's lodge. They knew it was a gift from Bear.

When it was her time, the woman went to the other side.

The people say a big black bear came and sat with her body for three days. They say the bear told stories and sang wonderful old songs.

Turd Man

RED LEGS was a strong, young man. Many women in his village wanted to share their lodge with him. But he had only one woman on his mind and she ignored him.

Star was exceptionally attractive and she knew it. She also knew that Red Legs loved her. So, she flirted with every man in the village except him.

One day Red Legs followed Star to the river where she often bathed or sat alone singing, for she had a lovely voice. He hid behind a great cedar and played a love song on his flute.

At last she called, "That's such a beautiful song, Red Legs. Please, play it again."

Of course, Red Legs was greatly encouraged and played the song several times before creeping quietly away. This was the first time Star had given him any reason to believe that she might be interested in him.

One night he brought a side of fresh venison to her lodge. She thanked him and followed him out into the moonlight to hold his hand and thank him for the good gift. She danced around him and kissed him on the nose.

Red Legs went home with a pounding heart and a flushed face. He couldn't sleep. His mother worried. His father scowled.

"That vain young woman will not be a good wife for my son," his anxious mother thought.

His father was thinking, too. "Star has every man in the village after her. I wish she'd leave Red Legs alone. If he gets stuck with her, he'll never be happy."

Red Legs' parents tried to discourage the romance with prayers and stares.

Star knew they didn't like to see her with their son. She knew that they thought ill of her and she didn't like them much, either.

So, one day, as the young couple was walking through the village, Star stopped and began shouting at Red Legs.

"When we're married," she said in a loud voice, "I hope you won't play that pitiful love song on that tired old flute you carry in your ragged bag."

Red Legs was surprised. "I thought you liked that song."

"I hope you don't try to win my affection with rotten deer meat," she went on.

"You must know I'd never do such a thing."

"I can have any man I want. So I've decided that I won't marry you, after all. I will choose a man more handsome than you. My husband must be an exceptional flute player and a mighty hunter." Then she walked off, leaving him alone, in shock and confusion.

Of course, Red Legs was terribly humiliated by Star's loud insults. He turned from the retreating woman and walked quickly to his parent's lodge. Then he packed a bundle of food and went to a small cave far from the village, where he could consider the matter without further distraction.

Because she'd deliberately led him on and given him hope that she cared for him, he found her conduct unforgivable. So the deeply wounded young man began to plot against the beautiful woman he'd once loved.

One night he returned to the village and gathered the turds he found in the shallow pits that were used for poop.

He carried the poop to the cave and formed it into a man. He made him tall, slender and handsome. Then he left the turd man to cure.

Afterwards, he went to a nearby village and hired a woman to make a quilled shirt and leggings. He went to a second village and found a woman who agreed to quill an apron and a jacket for him. Then he went to a third village where a woman quilled a pair of moccasins, a pair of gloves and a fur-lined hood. During this time Red Legs carved a beautiful cedar flute and made a fine otter skin bag to carry it in.

After a long while, Red Legs dressed the turd man in the fine new clothes. Then he pressed a red stone into the turd man's navel and he came to life. Cautiously he sat up, rubbed his hands together and felt his beautiful face. Then he stood up and stumbled around the cave on his new legs. Soon, he was strutting about proudly.

Then Red Legs showed Turd Man how to play the flute. Soon he was able to play beautifully and one frosty evening they returned to Red Legs' village.

When Star saw the two young men arrive together, she asked Red Legs, "Who's your good-looking friend?"

"Sleeping Bear," he replied. Then he brushed past her and walked away without another word.

Of course, Star thought Red Legs was jealous and she began flirting with "Sleeping Bear" in a most outrageous manner. Then she followed him through the village to Red Leg's lodge.

When the door flap was closed against her, she returned to her own lodge to dream of the handsome young stranger.

Inside Red Leg's lodge one of the children said, "Phew! Someone stepped in poop and carried it in on their moccasins."

Everyone looked at "Sleeping Bear." He was so embarrassed by his unpleasant odor that he excused himself and went outside. He sat behind the lodge and played the flute.

Star heard the beautiful music floating through the darkness. Of course, she imagined it was a love song he played only for her.

"Sleeping Bear" slept on the ground behind the lodge that night. Several of the village dogs came and lay down with him. He was grateful for their warmth.

The next day Star, dressed in her finest outfit, went to Red Legs' lodge and asked to see Sleeping Bear.

She was surprised to hear that he was sleeping behind the lodge. Quickly she went around and found him cuddled up with several dogs. She chased the dogs away and shook "Sleeping Bear" until he woke up.

"Because of my beauty," she told the young man, "many men desire that I share my lodge with them. But I have chosen you. We will be married tomorrow."

Without waiting for a response she hurried away.

Later that day she told her mother to prepare a marriage feast.

Then Star built a new lodge nearby.

After they were married, "Sleeping Bear" refused to enter Star's lodge because he knew that if he sat in the warmth with her, he'd begin to stink.

"She'll complain," he worried, "and I'll be embarrassed."

At first Star was amused. "Don't be shy," she teased.

She tugged on his arms and tickled him. But he would not let himself be taken into the lodge.

Star was humiliated because everyone was laughing at her.

"Come inside now!" she yelled at her reluctant husband. "If you don't do as I say, I'll get my brothers to whip you, and in the morning I'll send you back to Red Legs' lodge. You'll be laughed at for the rest of your life."

"Sleeping Bear" said nothing. He simply turned and hurried away from his beautiful wife.

Star ran after him begging him to return. "Please, come back," she wept. "I'm sorry! I love you too much to let my brothers hurt you. I only said that to make you come into the lodge."

But "Sleeping Bear" kept walking. He went out of the village and into the forest.

His wife followed.

He walked up a stony hill.

She followed.

"Sleeping Bear" walked much faster than Star and soon he had left her far behind.

It was getting dark when she stumbled over something. She reached down and found her husband's glove. It was full of turds. She couldn't understand how poop had gotten into the glove but she shook it out and wiped the glove clean. Then she stuffed it with grass and carried it along.

Then she stumbled over the other glove. It was full of turds, too.

"Why would anyone put turds in my husband's gloves?" she wondered as she shook the poop out, stuffed the second glove with grass and carried it along.

Not far from there she found one of his moccasins full of poop. A little beyond that place, she found the other moccasin full of turds. She was baffled. But she cleaned them carefully, filled them with grass and carried them long.

"When I catch up to my husband I'll return them," she decided. "I know he'll appreciate my thoughtfulness and he'll probably forgive me, too."

At the top of the hill she found his leggings. A few feet down the other side, she found his apron and jacket. They were smeared with—poop. She scraped the garments clean, rolled them into a bundle with the other clothing and carried it along.

At last she found the fur-lined hood with Turd Man's beautiful face smiling up at her in the moonlight.

Star screamed, dropped the bundle of fine clothes and ran back toward the village.

When she returned to her lodge she went inside and refused to come out. She remained in seclusion for a long, long time. Every night her mother brought food and placed it beside the door. In the morning the food was gone.

Red Legs went off to live with his father's relatives in a distant village and he soon found a good wife.

When Star finally left her lodge, she'd been transformed into a patient, considerate, respectful young woman.

Later she became the wife of a good man and raised three respectful daughters.

A Jealous Husband

IT HAPPENED in the long ago that a man married a widow with a little boy of two winters.

The woman loved her child so much that the man became jealous and grew to hate him.

One night the little boy was not ready to eat when his meal was served. The man and his wife ate, but the child did not.

Then the man said, "Don't feed the boy until tomorrow, because he would not eat with us."

Later that night the boy was hungry and cried for food. The man became angry and put the child outside the lodge. He tied the door shut and told his wife not to open it.

But the woman pitied the little one, so she crept past her husband and tried to open the door. He caught her and held her down. When she begged him to allow her to go out and sit with her son, he struck her with a piece of firewood.

When she awakened she heard the child's screams growing more and more faint. She knew that the owls had carried him away.

The next morning her husband went out to hunt. He didn't even mention the little one.

After he left, the woman went out looking for her baby. At last she found a place where a small skull and little bones were scattered about. Quickly she gathered them all up, built a fire and laid the bones in the blaze. Soon the bones were reduced to ashes.

She picked up the ashes, wrapped them in a bundle and carried them home. She prepared a meal for her husband and sprinkled it with the ashes from the bones of her little boy.

When the hungry man returned, she put the food before him and he ate it. He finished with a loud burp, a sneeze and a cough.

Then he laid down to rest. After a while she looked at him. His eyes were open and his mouth moved, but he could not speak. It wasn't long before he died.

She stayed with him until the next morning, then packed all her things, the ashes and her baby's belongings in her basket and carried it outside the lodge.

Then she laid dry wood around the lodge and burned it down.

She walked to another village where she found two of her younger brothers.

They were surprised to see her alone and asked about the boy.

At first she could only weep. Finally she told them everything.

One of them said, "It's a good thing he died, for we surely would have killed him."

The other one said, "Stay with us. We'll take care of you."

So they lived together until the end of their lives.

Four Little Men

IT HAPPENED during a period of low water on the shores of Lake Winnibigoshish that several piles of broken agates and flint were discovered. In the piles were arrowheads that had apparently been discarded by craftsmen as being less than perfect. The interesting thing about these arrowheads was that they were all quite small.

Because of the mysterious nature of the tiny arrowheads, a certain man decided to go in search of the arrowhead makers and find out who they were. So it was that one night he came upon four little men crafting arrowheads in a most peculiar manner.

They had built a small fire and prepared a bed of very hot coals. In the coals they laid many small red agates. When the stones were hot the little men removed them from the heat and laid them on the sand. Then they dipped a feather into a pot of water and touched the feather to the edge of the stone. A tiny ping was heard as a sliver of stone snapped off.

When the stones cooled, they were returned to the fire and others were taken. So the little men worked together through the night. This went on until they had created a handful of exquisite, incredibly tiny, arrowheads.

As the sun came up, they gathered their arrowheads and slipped into the forest, disappearing almost instantly.

The curious man returned to the site several nights later and waited in a concealed area until the four little men returned.

He was surprised to see them approaching in a small stone boat with mythical iconic symbols carved on the side of the vessel. The boat was round and one little man paddled, while the other three sat quietly holding their pots and feathers.

When they went ashore they built a fire and set to work. Once again he watched them make their tiny arrowheads.

Although the presence of the little people is widely known, they are rarely seen. So when the young man returned to his village, he told what he had seen. Several of his friends were eager to see the little stone workers for themselves.

So the next night the man returned with several friends, but although they waited all night, the little men did not appear. On subsequent nights some of the curious men returned alone. But the little men had vanished.

Although many people have seen the abandoned sites of chipped agate and flint, no one ever saw the little men again.

They are elusive and secretive people who do not wish to become spectacles for those who are merely curious about them.

Those who seek the Little People often interfere with their work by forcing them into hiding or causing them to abandon old sites and search for new ones.

Buffalo Wife

WHEN THE LAND was full of buffalo, the two-leggeds hunted them for food, clothing, tools and shelter.

However, the two-leggeds were careful to take no more than they needed and had respect for the lives of the buffalo who died. For two-leggeds knew it was the buffalo who enabled them to survive.

But it happened that the two-leggeds grew careless and forgot to teach their children how important it was to honor the Buffalo Nation. So there grew up a generation who did not respect the buffalo. They hunted beyond their need and often allowed much buffalo to be wasted.

So the Buffalo Nation called a council and decided that they would no longer give up their lives for the two-leggeds. They would no longer allow themselves to be killed to provide food, clothes and shelter for the ungrateful ones.

It wasn't long before the two-leggeds grew hungry and ragged. They offered all manner of prayers to Creator concerning their pitiful condition, but still they were not allowed to take a buffalo life.

One day, a young woman went to get water and saw a herd of buffalo standing on a high rocky ridge. She called to them. "Oh, buffalo brothers and sisters, we are hungry! Soon winter will be upon us and we will starve.

Only with your help can we hope to continue to survive!"

She was so concerned for the welfare of her people that she made a desperate promise. She shouted, "If some of you will fall down and give your lives that my people might live, I will marry a buffalo!"

To her surprise, several buffalo stepped over the rocky ridge and plunged to their deaths on the stones below. She ran to the village and told the other women what had happened. They followed her to the place where the buffalo lay dead.

How excited they were as they skinned the buffalo and carried the meat home! That night there was much to celebrate! The people sang and danced and told stories!

The following day, the young woman was on her way to get water when she met a great bull buffalo.

"Come with me," he told her. "I am your husband."

But she did not want to be the wife of a buffalo. So she said, "Please allow me to go home and say goodbye to my family and my many friends."

"Very well," the buffalo said. "But tomorrow, when the sun stands high in the sky, you must return to this place. I will be waiting. If you do not return, it will be as it was before. Buffalo did not allow themselves to be killed by your people. Your people will starve."

Then he wheeled about and returned to his nation.

The young woman returned to her home and told her parents everything. She said she didn't want to be married to a buffalo.

Her parents understood. However, there was the promise that she had given. It could not be ignored.

After long consideration, her father said, "Daughter, you must go to your buffalo husband. You made a promise. You gave your word. If you do not return to him, our people will starve."

So she packed a basket of things she would need and went to meet her husband. She followed him across the land.

It was a long and difficult winter, but now the two-leggeds had everything they needed to survive.

In the spring the father began thinking about his daughter and told his wife he was going to find her.

His wife knew better. "No," she told him. "If you try to bring our daughter home that buffalo will kill you!"

But the man said, "I will not try to bring her home. I only want to see her. I want to know if she is well. I want to know if that buffalo is kind to her."

Seeing that he would not be dissuaded, the woman made him ready for his journey and he went out to look for their daughter.

He searched all along the waterways and shallow wallows looking for her tracks. He found nothing. But on his way back to the village, he discovered a shallow water hole where the fresh tracks of a young woman mingled with the tracks of many buffalo. He knew that she was near, so he hid himself behind some rocks and waited to see if she would return.

Not far from there, the buffalo were grazing on sweet spring grass.

The buffalo husband said to his wife, "My throat is dusty. I'm thirsty and I'm tired. I want you to go to the water hole and bring me some water."

So the woman took her water bag and went to get water for her husband. Her father saw her coming and ran to meet her. What a happy reunion they had!

But after some time the woman said, "I must return to my husband."

"No," her father said. "Please, come home with me."

"I cannot," the woman said. "The welfare of all our people is in my hands."

When she left, her father hid behind the rocks again. He thought, "When she returns, I'll tell her how lonely her mother is. I'll tell her how much we need her. I'm sure she can be persuaded to come home with me then."

When she returned to her buffalo husband and put the water bag down for him to drink, the bull snorted, stamped his hoof and said, "I smell a two-legged!"

The woman said, "You smell me."

"I smell another two-legged!" the furious buffalo bellowed. "What kind of a woman are you? You went to the waterhole to meet a two-legged!"

"I went to the waterhole to get water for you," she reminded him.

But he pawed the earth with his great black hooves and tossed his head in anger. "That two-legged will die!" he roared.

Then he gathered a few other buffalo and went to find and kill the two-legged. They trampled his remains until there was nothing left of him.

When the woman arrived, she fell down weeping in the place where her father's blood stained the earth.

The buffalo husband did not pity his wife. Her tears only infuriated him. "If I were dead, you would not mourn for me! Who was this two-legged?" the buffalo husband wanted to know.

The woman stood up before his great bull head and said, "The two-legged whom you killed was my father."

The buffalo was surprised, but he was still angry. "Do you grieve when the buffalo are killed so that your people can live?"

"My people perish, too," she said.

Now the buffalo began to pity the woman and her people. "Here's what we will do," he said. "If you can bring your father back to life, we buffalo will continue to allow ourselves to be killed by your people. But when you kill a buffalo you must honor that buffalo with a dance. If you do this, the spirit of the buffalo who died will be reborn in a buffalo calf and so there will always be buffalo."

So the woman got down on her knees in that muddy bloody place and began searching for a piece of her father's body that hadn't been crushed or broken by the buffalo.

As she searched, a magpie came along and asked her why she was digging in the bloody mud. She explained everything to the bird.

Then the bird said, "I will help you."

So it was that the bird found a piece of her father's backbone that had not been crushed or broken and laid it in the woman's hand.

She thanked the bird for his help and carried the vertebra to the top of a high grassy hill and covered it with her buffalo robe. She sang and prayed for four days and three nights and when she raised the robe, there was her father's body, completely restored. But he was dead.

So she covered the body and began to sing and pray again. Soon, she raised the robe and her father opened his eyes.

Then he stood up and they walked back to where the bull was waiting.

When the buffalo saw the power his wife had, he released her from the marriage. He showed daughter and father how to honor the Buffalo Nation with a dance and trotted away to rejoin the herd.

The man and his daughter returned to the village, told the people what had happened and taught them how to do the buffalo honoring dance.

As a result of this young woman's efforts to protect the welfare of her people, many nations still benefit from the life of the buffalo. Because many people continue to do this dance, there are still buffalo on Turtle Island.

However, when people hear this story they sometimes scoff and declare, "Buffalo do not speak to people! Animals can't talk!"

But as a wise old woman once said, "You do not mean to say that buffalo do not speak to people. What you really mean to say is that a buffalo has not yet spoken to *you*!"

The First Teller

T HERE WAS A TIME in the long ago when there were no storytellers among the First Nations of Turtle Island.

But on a cold winter day a young hunter, who had been allowed to kill three partridges and four rabbits to provide much-needed food for his extended family, had a strange experience as he went along toward home.

Although the boy was strong, he suddenly became exhausted. Soon he was having so much difficulty lifting his feet to move forward that he decided to rest.

As he sat in the shelter of a great stone waiting for his strength to return, he heard a voice. The boy looked carefully about, but there was no one to be seen.

Of course, he became somewhat alarmed and shouted, "Who are you? What do you want?"

The voice answered, "I am the great stone and I want to tell you a story."

When the boy looked more closely at the stone, he saw a huge face looking back at him.

Then he sat down and waited.

After a few minutes he said, "I'm ready to hear your story."

But the stone replied, "A story is a gift. If I give you a gift, you must give me a gift, too."

The boy had nothing to offer but his small game. He thought of his hungry family, sitting in the lodge, waiting for food. But the stone had asked for a gift and could not be refused. Therefore, the boy tossed two partridges and a rabbit up on top of the stone.

"Thank you, my son," the stone said.

Then the stone told a wonderful story and soon the boy forgot that it was winter. He forgot that the snow was getting deeper and deeper in the forest, making it difficult for the hunter and the hunted. He forgot that the cold wind was driving the snow against the lodges in his village. He forgot that frost was gathering on the inside walls of his family's lodge. He forgot that their food supply was shrinking and would soon be gone. He forgot how the children would cry for food, how the mothers would weep, how the old ones would suffer. He forgot how the hunters would mourn because they could not provide for their people. As the boy listened to the story that the stone told, he forgot all of these things.

When the story was completed, the boy thanked the stone and returned to his village.

That night he gathered his friends and family in his mother's lodge and told the story the stone had shared with him.

As the people listened they forgot that hunting had been poor that day. They forgot that the wind was howling around the lodge. They forgot that the snow was piling up outside. They forgot that many infants and elders would not live to see the new green spring. As they listened to the story that the boy told, they forgot all of the things that had troubled them before.

Afterwards they thanked the boy and went to their own lodges. Some of them discussed the wonderful story before they went to sleep.

The next evening they asked the boy to tell the story again.

Several sleeps later the boy went hunting and took an offering of four partridges to the stone.

Then he sat down to hear another story of wonder and magic. Once more he forgot the troubles that his people were facing.

Later, he repeated the story and for a while, his people forgot their difficulties and their concerns for the future.

Every few sleeps the boy went to the stone with a gift and heard a new story, which he repeated to the people.

Then, as the green shoots were emerging, the boy went to the stone, gave his offering and sat down. But the stone did not speak.

"I have come to hear a story," the boy called.

The stone said, "You have heard all my stories. I have no more stories to tell. These are my gifts to you. Now, I want you to make new ones."

Then the stone encouraged the boy with a great and wonderful truth. "You are a storyteller! Where there are storytellers, there will be stories and where there are stories, there will be storytellers."

The Woman Who Made Drums

I T HAPPENED early one morning long ago that men who came from the north invaded a certain village that stood near Father Waters in the midst of Turtle Island.

The dawn attack was swift and terrible. The old people of the village tried to hide in their lodges, those with strength ran into the woods, young mothers fell down with their arms around their children. No one expected mercy—and none was given.

But one young woman had run into the river and stood among the rushes, breathing through a hollow reed. There she remained all day and into the long night.

As she stood in the cold, black water, she considered what terrible things had happened to her people. At last she was overwhelmed by grief and despair. So she decided that she would go with them to the other side.

Suddenly she heard someone speaking to her. The voice told her that she would not be killed. She would live! She would go forth and remind all peoples of the Original Instructions.

The people would rediscover how they could live in peace, harmony and balance. They would find within themselves all they needed to live well and prosper. Nations would no longer fight other nations for territory, resources and status.

"But war is inevitable," the woman reasoned. "It has always been so, and always so it shall be."

"No," the voice sadly answered, "it has not. But many things have been forgotten. But I will show you a better way. I will teach you the way of peace."

Then it was that the woman received a vision of twelve drums. She'd seen drums before, small personal hand drums like the men in her village carried about with them. But these new drums were so large that several men could gather around them. These drums had great voices, too.

In the vision she saw herself going across the land to live among the peoples of many nations. She watched herself gather materials for the construction of the drums she dreamed. One by one she made them. The people listened to her words and, as work on the drum progressed, they learned the way of peace.

"Now you must leave the water," the voice told her.

"I will certainly be killed," the woman thought.

"No one will see you," the voice promised. "You will walk in the midst of these powerful invaders and you will not be harmed. You will live to make the drums you saw in your vision."

So the woman rose up from the water, walked through the village and went out into the nations. The enemy did not see her pass among them.

She lived a long and prayerful life dedicated to the creation of sacred drums.

In the end she made twelve. Then she was called to the other side. So twelve great nations were reminded of the Original Instructions and learned to live in peace, harmony and balance.

Then it happened that powerful men from far away—carried over the great salt waters by large swimming birds—invaded Turtle Island.

These men had no knowledge of the Original Instructions and no respect for the message of peace, harmony and balance.

After many years there was no place on Turtle Island where their feet had not touched. Everywhere they went, they carried greed, corruption, violence and death.

Of course, the woman had warned the twelve nations that such peoples would arrive. She'd told them the newcomers would bring vile spirits. These spirits would live in the firewater the invaders carried.

"You must not drink this," she'd told them again and again.

But after several generations, her words had been forgotten and the vile spirits that lived in the firewater had enslaved the many First Nations peoples of Turtle Island.

Then it happened that the drums began to disappear.

One day they were in the midst of the people—and the next day they were gone!

But in that place where the woman had made the first drum, an elder man remembered her words of warning. He'd heard them from his father, who'd heard them from his mother, who'd heard them from her father.

He had been told, "When these vile spirits come to this nation, you must protect the drum. You will do this by remembering the songs of this drum. You will carry the drum out to the arbor every morning. You will sing and pray. On a certain night you will dream. Then Creator will give you a vision of what must be done to protect the drum—and you will do it."

So it happened one day that the drum was silent. The people who lived in that village awakened under a dark sky and found that their sacred drum was gone!

But this ancient drum had not disappeared. The elder man had hidden it. Where? No one knows. For when he passed over, he took the secret with him. He could not disclose its location to anyone, for the spirits that lived in the firewater that the invaders had brought to the village had defiled many.

But somewhere in the heart of Turtle Island, an infant has been born. This little one is growing in strength and knowledge. Here is a child of wisdom and courage. Here is a child who will dream a dream. This child will remember the Original Instructions.

Perhaps this one will find the last sacred drum. Perhaps this one will create a new one. But what will surely be done is this: The child will mature and go out to teach other nations.

Many will listen, some will hear, and a few will choose the way of peace, harmony and balance. Others will continue to endure the captivity brought to First Nations peoples by the newcomers who arrived long ago on the wings of great floating birds.

It might happen that the teacher will be harassed for failing to conform to the lesser expectations of a people who have lost their Original Instructions and have no respect for messengers of peace, harmony and balance.

It might happen that the teacher will be accepted and the people will treasure the Original Instructions. They will learn to walk in peace, harmony and balance, and the song of sacred drums will once again welcome the dawn.

Seven Daughters

IT HAPPENED long ago that a certain man lived near a long point of land with his four wives and seven daughters. The point of land went some distance into the lake, which was so big it was difficult to see the other shore. A large water serpent frequently visited this lake.

The serpent had invariably appeared at the birthing of each of the seven daughters. Therefore, everyone knew that they would grow into exceptional women.

As infants they were not remarkable but by the time they reached their seventh winter, each girl had become a shape-shifter.

The children were raised by Beaver standards. So they were kind, generous, intelligent, patient, compassionate, industrious, clean, brave, frugal and territorial.

They became excellent hunters, trappers and warriors. So they were able to supply their family and extended family and others with game and food and skins. They went out with the male warriors to confront anyone who entered their territory without their consent. So the man was pleased with his daughters and never longed for sons.

Sometimes the man, his wives and their daughters would get into their canoes and paddle along the shores to visit relatives in other lakeside villages.

The family always felt safe. They lived beyond danger in a time of peace.

But one day their relatives told them dreadful stories of violent white intruders. None of these people had seen the intruders but stories of their strange behavior traveled from the east. They say the old ones had seen them coming in their dreams. So they decided to send scouts out to discover the truth of these frightening rumors.

Twenty-eight warriors were selected. Because of their exceptional abilities, the party included four of the warrior-sisters.

On the day appointed, the scouting party got into four well-equipped canoes and began their journey.

As they went along, they stopped to gather information about the intruders. It was always the same. They were hairy, foul-smelling brutes who attacked without cause and multiplied without women. They were bloodless monstrosities who had arrived on great floating birds. They were mindless murderers who butchered children.

The charges were unbelievable but after some time the scouts found themselves entering uninhabited villages. The people had panicked, abandoned their homes and fled without resistance.

Then they came upon villages where bodies of children, women, and men rotted on the ground. Only their scalps had been taken. This was most disturbing, for such butchery was unknown among First Nations. They were sickened by such vicious savagery.

"What manner of men do such things?" they wondered.

They went on with extreme caution and eventually discovered a village of houses constructed by the intruders. They could smell the brutes long before they saw them. Two of the women and two men were sent for a closer look.

At one point one of the women was seen by an intruder. When he attempted to pursue her she shape-shifted into a spider and hid on a tree trunk. The intruder was baffled and frightened by her sudden disappearance.

The four scouts returned with disturbing news. They were badly outnumbered and could not advise an attack. So it was decided that they had seen enough and should return home to warn their people about the barbaric intruders.

The white intruder began spreading the story about the disappearing woman. No one believed him because he was a disreputable liar incapable of speaking truth.

Then it happened that after four winters, reports of the white intruders surfaced close to their peaceful village and the people prepared for an assault. But these white brutes wanted to trade cloth, cooking pots, iron knife blades and beads for beaver pelts.

When the traders were seen approaching, the wives and daughters hurried out to the point as planned. But several vulgar white traders saw the seven daughters and lusted for them.

After the bargaining was complete, the traders were sent away because no one wanted them to remain in or near the village. They were not only foul smelling, but their conduct was grossly offensive to the people of the village.

But it happened that several of the traders plotted how they would capture the women and take them away for their own vile pleasure. So on the following day when the traders returned for more business, the vulgar men climbed up on the backside of the peninsula and concealed themselves until the man, his wives and four brothers left.

The father looked back several times and seeing nothing amiss returned to the village to continue bargaining for trade goods. He posted his four wives as sentries, but they wanted to look at the calico fabric the traders had brought. So for a few minutes, they were distracted.

The wind was blowing in from the lake and the water was crashing along the peninsula so the women didn't hear the men creeping toward them.

Suddenly the vulgar men rose up and were seen by the older women who set up a keening song. Then the voices of all the women were raised, the children pointed toward the peninsula and the good men of the village shouted as they ran to help.

The vulgar men rushed at the young women, who ran like deer and were soon hidden in the woods. The men plunged in after them.

The women shape-shifted into mice and hid under the leaves. When the vulgar men couldn't find the women, they remembered the story of the disappearing woman.

With the whole village after them, the vulgar men had to leave.

But when traders returned the following year, the vulgar men accompanied them. Now they had a new plan for seizing the women.

When the father lined his daughters up on the peninsula, their uncles and the other good men of the village searched diligently for any intruders who might be hidden along the shore. When they were satisfied that the intruders were not present they returned to the village to bargain for trade goods.

But the vulgar men had posted themselves in the forest and sent three along the peninsula to frighten the women.

When the women ran into the forest the men were waiting. After much screaming and pathetic pleading, the women emerged unharmed. However, the vulgar men were never seen again.

They say when the women entered the forest they shape-shifted into cougars. Quickly they grabbed the vulgar men by the throats with their powerful jaws and crushed their vertebrae. The smell of blood attracted several hungry wolves who dragged the bodies away. Soon the carcasses were devoured.

It is said that when the frightened traders left with their plunder, the sea serpent pursued them across the lake. Like their vulgar companions, they were never seen again.

So the seven daughters and their children lived beyond danger in a time of peace, for it was many years before any white traders ventured back to that place.

Woman Lake

T HERE WAS ONCE A MAN who had two wives. Although they were sisters, they shared very few characteristics and had little in common. One was tall, one was short. One was plump, one was thin. One was quiet, one was loud. One was rude, one was kind. One was energetic, and one tired easily.

One wife was called Weasel, the other was Beaver.

Weasel was quick-tempered and anxious, while Beaver was placid and gentle.

Beaver had been a first wife. Weasel became the second wife when her parents had both crossed over and she was left alone. The man had hoped that the two women would help one another and be an encouragement to him. His father had married sisters, too. The man remembered the unwavering friendship shared by his two mothers.

But Weasel was disagreeable and confrontational. She often accused their husband of loving Beaver more than he loved her. While it was true that the man preferred the companionship of Beaver, his love for the women was equal. He tried not to favor Beaver, but Weasel became angry anyway. This made life difficult for everyone.

It happened one day that the man went out to hunt and saw two otters playing on the riverbank. "I'll take two otters home today," he thought. "One for each of the women."

Creeping close, he killed one with an arrow, while the other escaped into the water. The man set a snare and returned home.

He gave the otter to Beaver because she was first wife and told Weasel what had happened. Of course, she didn't believe him.

"You brought an otter for Beaver. But for me you have only excuses!" she complained.

The following day the man returned to the river to check the snare. He found it empty and set another nearby. But when he arrived home without an otter, Weasel was angry.

"What!" she shouted, "no gift for your beloved Beaver?"

Beaver said nothing but sat on her mat scraping the otter hide. Weasel's resentment and anger made life difficult for the rest of them.

Every day the poor man went out to search for another otter so that Weasel would stop quarreling with him. But every day he returned with nothing and there was no peace in his lodge.

One day Weasel told Beaver, "I can't stand this any longer. I won't live in the same lodge with you. I hate you. I want our husband for myself. Go away!"

Beaver did not argue, she simply refused to go away. "This is my home, too," she reminded her sister.

"Then we must have contest," Weasel said. "We will swim around the small lake near our village. We will stay in the water until one of us drowns. The one who survives will have our husband to herself."

Beaver did not want to do this, but Weasel insisted.

Weasel ran to the lake, stripped and jumped in. Reluctantly, Beaver followed.

Around and around they swam. Each time Weasel passed Beaver, she shouted, "I hate you!"

Beaver was weeping as she swam. She did not want to live in the unhappy lodge. Nor did she want anyone to drown. So she decided that she would leave and allow Weasel to have her way.

"I will go to my mother's sister," she thought. "She will understand how this has happened because she knows Weasel. I will ask her if I can live there. She will talk to her husband. I will offer to help make their lives easier."

Beaver crawled up on the shore. She sat for several minutes to catch her breath. Then she walked home to pack her belongings. When all was ready, she sat down to wait for Weasel. Soon it was nearly dark and still Weasel had not returned.

"She probably went to hide in the woods," Beaver told herself. "I will prepare a meal for our husband before I leave."

Later, when the man came home, Beaver told him everything. While he was heartsick that his gentle wife was leaving, he wasn't going to stand in her way.

"You must do what you must do," he told her. "But first we must find Weasel. Perhaps she has changed her mind."

They searched all night but did not find her. Several days later some elder women found her body caught in their fishing net.

So Beaver and her husband lived a peaceful life together and the people named the lake, Jealous Woman Lake. Today it is called Woman Lake, but almost everyone has forgotten why.

The Stone

A CERTAIN MAN lived near a field. In the middle of the field was a great stone. The man called the stone "Grandfather" because it had stood in the field for many, many winters.

Now it happened one day that the man was hungry and there was no food in his lodge. He sat for a long time, hugging his belly and moaning in a loud pitiful voice.

Then he decided he would go to the stone and pray for food. He wrapped his old robe around him and hurried to the field.

He laid himself upon the stone. "Grandfather," he wept, "I am hungry. Truly, I am starving! Please give me something to eat. Provide me with meat."

As he lay there he began to feel very warm. Then he began to perspire.

He decided that he didn't need the old robe anymore. So he sweetened his prayer with an offering.

"Grandfather, I know you have heard my prayer. I know you will provide meat for me. So I'm giving you my robe."

Then the man spread the robe over the stone with a grand gesture and went away.

Now Great Spirit is not a stone, but Great Spirit is in all places at all times. Therefore, Great Spirit had heard and seen what the man had said and done.

As the man walked along his way he came upon a freshly killed deer. He looked about, but there was no one else around.

Then he smiled and raised happy hands toward the red sky of the setting sun.

"Thank you, Grandfather!" he shouted. "You have provided the meat I need."

The man skinned the deer and cut off a hindquarter. He laid the wood for a fire and prepared to cook his venison.

But he could not light the fire. No matter how he tried, the tinder would not kindle.

By now it was getting dark and he could feel the cold creeping over his neck, his shoulders and his back. His teeth began to chatter. Still, he could not light the fire.

Suddenly he stood up and threw down his flint.

"I need my robe," he thought. "Grandfather doesn't feel the cold. He doesn't need a robe."

So the man returned to the field and pulled the robe from the stone.

Now Great Spirit is not a stone. But Great Spirit is in all places at all times. Therefore, it was Great Spirit who had provided the meat for the hungry man.

Quickly the man wrapped himself in his robe and returned to his camp. What he saw stopped him dead in his tracks. His mouth fell open!

The venison was gone! Where the fresh deer had been, there was a skeleton! He couldn't believe his eyes! He touched the ribs. They were dry as sticks.

The man fell down. He hugged his belly and moaned sadly.

But instead of being sorry for what he'd done, he said, "I should have eaten all the meat before I took back my robe."

Now the man had shown how selfish and lazy he was. So Great Spirit, who heard the cries of the hungry man, paid no attention to them.

Then the man got up and said, "I will go to my sister. Her husband is a good hunter. She will have meat. I'll trade her something for it. Maybe my old robe. I won't need it tomorrow when it's warm again."

Hunter

Long ago there was an outstanding hunter. No matter the season or the weather, he always returned from the hunt with game.

Then it was that he became great with pride and was often heard boasting of his abilities and belittling those who had experienced little or no success.

He was also quite selfish. He thought only of himself and his own household, ignoring the hungry people around him.

One day as the men were preparing to leave for a hunt, he shouted, "I will certainly return with a great deer, or a moose, or even a bear. Perhaps you other men would like me to show you how to hunt. It's doubtful that any of you will ever surpass me, but your families would be thankful for more than an occasional rabbit and a few skinny partridges."

Oh, how he ridiculed his neighbors.

Indeed, it was Creator who had blessed the man with such great skill. But now Creator decided it was time to teach this man an important lesson. So when the man went out to hunt that day, he did not see any game. He did not even find any animal tracks. It seemed the game had disappeared.

Then as the sun began to set, he realized that he would not return to his village with a deer, a moose, or a bear, so he decided to settle for a few rabbits. But not even a rabbit crossed his path that day.

The man remembered his loud boasting and couldn't face the other men. So he made camp and spent the night alone in the forest.

The next day he hunted again. Once more, he had no success. So he decided to spend another night in the forest and get up early to start hunting the next day.

"Surely tomorrow I'll have better luck," he thought.

When he awakened in the morning he was surprised to find an elder woman sitting nearby.

"Good morning, my son," she greeted him. "I see you still have nothing to eat after hunting for several days. Of course, you must be too ashamed to go home now. I'm sure you're quite hungry, too. Follow me and I will take you to my lodge where I have plenty of food."

So the man got up and followed her.

They went a great distance and the man became quite tired, but the elder woman walked quickly and was soon far ahead of him.

At last he called to her, "Grandmother, I think we should stop here so you can rest for awhile."

"Why?" the woman replied. "I'm not tired."

So the man admitted that he was quite exhausted. "I cannot go on."

While they sat resting, the woman seemed to be staring at him. He was uncomfortable and asked, "Why do you look at me with such hard eyes?"

"I'm sorry," the woman said. "But I was wondering what kind of a man fills his belly every day and has no pity for his hungry neighbors."

The man didn't like to hear that, but he said nothing and soon they were on their way again.

At last they reached the woman's lodge.

The man was surprised to find that the woman lived alone. He wondered who hunted for her as she was an old woman and didn't carry a weapon.

"Sit down," the woman said when they got inside the lodge. She quickly built a fire.

The man looked around. He saw no food in the lodge and had not seen a storehouse when they arrived. So he wondered where she would get the food she'd promised to give him.

Soon the woman sat down across from him and took three small cooking pots from her belt-bag. She filled them with water and put them near the fire. When the water was steaming, she took a kernel of rice from the bag and put it into the first pot. Then she reached into the bag again and took out a small piece of dried fish, which she put in the second pot. Then she took out a mint leaf and put in the third pot.

When the rice was cooked, she gave the tiny pot to him and said, "Eat."

"Oh, no," the man said. "I can't take your last kernel of rice."

The woman laughed. "Take it," she said. "There will be plenty left for me."

So the man took the kernel of rice and placed it on his tongue. Carefully he bit into it. Oh, it was delicious. He wished there was more.

How surprised he was when he looked into the pot and saw another rice kernel waiting for him. Carefully he ate that one, too. Then another appeared. And so it went, until he was filled.

Then she gave him the fish. No matter how much he ate, there was always more. The same thing happened with the mint tea. The tiny pot was always full.

At last the woman asked, "Have you had enough, my son?"

"Yes," the man whispered.

Afterwards she gave the man a long look and said, "When you share what you have, you will find there is always enough."

Suddenly the man was waking up in his camp. Soon, a deer walked up to him and offered her life so he would have food.

The man returned to his village with enough meat to share with all his neighbors.

Finding Water

IT HAPPENED in a land already dry and full of dust that the sky people withheld the rain and the earth people suffered for there was not enough food to support all who lived there.

Scouts frequently went to search for a better place to live but they always returned, saying that all the land was dry. The people, afraid that conditions might become worse if they left, remained where they were—and they suffered for it. Well, you see, change is difficult.

But after four rainless years it had become impossible to live in the dry land. So the people prepared to leave. They had decided that if they were going to survive they would have to abandon their elders. Although they knew this would not be an easy decision, they felt it must be done and it must be done quickly.

Their plan was simple. Those who were strong enough would leave and those too weak to follow would be left behind. So they gave each elder a basket of bitter fruit and a scant amount of water. Then they moved on. It was a sorrowful people who did this thing and because they were ashamed, they did not look back. So the migration began.

Several of the elders stumbled along behind. They were able to follow for a few desperate miles but one by one they gave up and lay down to die.

One of the elder women who chose to remain in the empty village watched the old ones struggle until they were lost on the wavering horizon.

The woman lived there alone. She rationed her water carefully and ate hard-shelled beetles and nibbled at the bitter fruit. When there was nothing more to sustain her she prepared to die. Her death song was no more than a pathetic croak.

Then it happened as she lay down to wait for death that a strange bird came and, as the woman watched, began pecking at the earth with its long slender beak. All day and into the night the bird continued.

The weary woman fell asleep and in the morning she found that the bird had succeeded in digging a shallow depression in the sand. She decided to assist the bird and poked around in her basket until she found a small wooden spoon. Being too weak to walk, she crawled to the hole. When the bird stepped back she began digging. The bird watched her closely. After a while, the bird stepped forward and pecked. The woman took her turn again. So they continued in this manner, the woman and the bird.

At last the woman slept. In the morning she found that the bird had enlarged the hole considerably. So she took the spoon and resumed digging.

Then it was that a small amount of water bubbled up into the bottom of the hole. The woman began digging as quickly as she could and soon the hole was filled with good water. The bird bathed and the woman drank and washed her withered face.

Now her people had gone a considerable distance but had been unable to leave the dry land. No matter how far they walked they could not come to the end of the dusty hills. But suddenly one morning, the people saw a small stream of water flowing through their camp! Soon it was such an abundant flow that they were forced to seek higher ground.

After they had enjoyed the water, scouts went to discover the headwaters of the great life-giving river. They were amazed to find the elder woman— with the mysterious bird—sitting at the river's source.

She greeted the scouts kindly and asked if her children were well.

Soon, the others returned to find themselves welcomed and forgiven.

So it was that the elder woman became their Great Grandmother Water Guide. From then, generations of these people have been nourished and sustained, for they are always able to find good water.

The Dam

O NE DAY a certain nation of people who lived in the east of Turtle Island found that the river they relied on for water was drying up.

At first they said, "It will be all right. It's a temporary dry spell."

But soon the river became no more than a trickle and then it disappeared.

It wasn't long before the children were crying for water and the old ones were falling ill. So the people prayed for rain and a great storm followed. They filled every container they had and although they rationed it carefully, it was soon gone.

They prayed again and again, but no more rain fell.

"Something must be done," the grandmothers said.

So they sent a man up the river to find our what had happened to their water. It was a long journey and after several days he came to a village of prosperous people. He was surprised to discover that these people had stopped the river with a great dam. Behind the dam was a huge reservoir of water.

"Why have you done this?" he asked.

No one would answer.

But he repeated the question until a child crept close and whispered, "You must talk to our leader."

"Where can I find him?"

The child pointed toward a magnificent lodge that stood near the dam.

So the man hurried to the lodge where he discovered that the leader of these people was a giant toad who stood upright on thin crooked legs and walked with an ornately carved diamond willow cane. The toad looked at the man and blinked his lazy eyes. But he said nothing.

So the man spoke. "Why are you withholding water from my people? Surely you know we cannot live without water."

"What do I care?" the toad answered in a loud hoarse voice.

"Our children are dying!" cried the desperate man.

The toad smiled from ear to ear.

"We must have water. Please, have pity!" the man begged.

Suddenly the toad stepped out of the lodge and leaped to the top of the dam. Then he used his cane to dig a small hole in the dam. Soon a trickle of water was flowing down the river.

"There is your water," the toad said.

So the man returned to his village to find that a small amount of water had trickled down the old riverbed. The people rejoiced. But after a few sleeps, the trickle was gone and the river was dry again.

Then it happened that a mysterious man arrived at their village. He came suddenly, like the wind. He appeared among them, like magic.

He was exceptionally tall and wore many red feathers in his long black hair.

"I am here to help you," Red Feathers told the people. "Tell me what has happened."

So they told him how the giant toad had dammed the river and was withholding the water they needed to live.

"I will set this matter right," he promised.

Then he left.

He walked up the dry riverbed until he came to the village. Then he sat down to wait and while he waited, he sang. Soon a child crept close to get a better look at the newcomer.

"Please, get me a drink of water," Red Feathers said.

"I cannot," the child replied.

"Why not? You have more than enough."

"We cannot take water without asking the leader."

"Then go and ask him."

So the girl went and after quite a long time she returned with a small bowl of dirty water.

The man looked at the water and said, "I will see this leader for myself and he will soon be giving me more than just a little bowl of dirty water."

So he stood up and walked boldly toward the lodge.

Just as he reached the lodge, the giant toad leaped out and shouted, "What do you want?"

"Give me a drink of clean water, you thing of mud!"

But the toad shook his cane in Red Feathers' face and said, "Get out of here! Find water elsewhere! This water is mine!"

Quickly the man grabbed the cane and stuck it into the toad's belly. Mud gushed out of the wound. At that same moment, the dam collapsed and water began rushing down the riverbed.

The people of the village ran toward Red Feathers and he prepared to defend himself. But the people did not wish to hurt him. They wanted to thank him for getting rid of their dreadful leader.

When they looked at the great toad, they found that he was no larger than a person's head. So Red Feathers picked up the toad and crushed him in his hand. Then taking the cane, he dug a deep hole and buried the toad.

From that day to this, no toad has been allowed to grow larger than a person's fist.

The River

IT HAPPENED in the long, long ago that there was a certain nation of people who were troubled by vexing spirits. Some of these spirits were as small as fleas, and others were as large as deerflies. They say that a few were as big as the great moose.

Now, all theses spirits lived in the land of Look Behind. The land was called Look Behind because the spirits were always sneaking up behind the unhappy people who lived there.

Then the leaders of these people told everyone to walk backwards so they could see the spirits that buzzed about, stinging them and biting them, causing infection, sores and diseases. But no matter which way the people walked, the spirits were always behind them.

So some of the bold warriors, who wore proud courage feathers, made horrible masks to wear on the backs of their heads. Now, they were sure that the spirits could not tell if the two-faced men were coming or going.

But this did not help. In fact, it made things worse. You see, these spirits could not be fooled but they *could* be annoyed. Soon, they became irritated and angry. To show their displeasure, they put an eternal curse upon the people of Look Behind. So, from that day to this day, even beyond tomorrow, no one will ever trust any two-faced person.

At last, the troubled people of Look Behind decided to hold a great council meeting. The medicine men built the council fire of pine heartwood and kindled it with the youngest flame struck from the sacred flint.

They sprinkled the fire with tobacco and prayed for the vision of a lynx, the determination of a beaver, and the wisdom of a fox. They strongly desired that they see clearly what must be done to keep the spirits from harassing them. They must be strong in their resolve, and cunning in their thoughts.

The smoke hazed up and billowed out and grew up into a thick black cloud that covered the people of Look Behind, shutting them up in darkness. This was a terrible experience for the pitiful people. Of course, they were frightened.

But out of the cloud came Father Water, a sad and gentle giant. They say he was so big that no one had ever seen all of him at the same time.

In a voice as soft as the whisper of the wind, he spoke to the poor people crouched around the fire. He told them not to fear the vexing spirits of Look Behind. He told them that he would trap the spirits in lakes that he would scatter across the land. He told them that every lake would catch the spirits who wanted to torment the people.

He said, "These lakes will be filled with water from my own body. Then I must lie down and die. It is my wish that you and your people should care for my body forever. But it is for you and you alone to know that my heart-place will be a shallow lake." Then he disappeared, the council fire flickered out, the smoke lifted and the darkness was gone.

Now the people could see clearly. They had new confidence and were able to understand many things that had puzzled them before.

Now they looked out upon a new land of great beauty. The land was dotted with sparkling lakes, and through the land ran a mighty river, full of strength and abounding with life. They called the river Father of Waters. Today it is called the Mississippi.

The people traveled down the river and found the shallow place that Father Water called his heart-place. This is now called Lake Pepin.

The people chose this place for mourning and burying their dead. It is said that for hundreds of years they wrapped their dead in birch bark and took them down the river to burial sites along Lake Pepin.

They did this so they could be certain that their loved ones would lie forever in the heart-place of Father Water. They knew that as long as the people remembered to honor him, they would continue to live long and pleasant lives in a good land.

For countless generations, the children were instructed to respect the river. But now the great river is dying, and we who were charged to care for it seem powerless to prevent it. Others are unmoved by the plight we have brought upon ourselves by failing to respect the river and forgetting to honor Father Water.

Because we are no longer ignorant of the great harm that has been done to this mighty river, this gift from Father Water, we will pay a price. People all along the river will pay. Our children and our grandchildren will pay.

We see Father Water lying in his bed corrupted and defiled by those who exploit our resources. It is as though the purpose of the river is only to serve the careless, the ignorant, the unprincipled and greedy.

Surely this cannot be allowed to continue. Surely we have some leaders who can still see clearly, who understand what must be done, and who have the courage to stand up in defense of Father Water and declare, "Enough! It is enough! Stop destroying our river!"

It is time to let the river heal. It is time to honor Father Water just as the Old Ones did.

It is time to free Father Water from the pollution and contaminants that trouble our great river, just as Father Water freed the people from the spirits that troubled them in the long ago land of Look Behind.

Too Many Rules

LONG AGO, a certain nation grew resentful toward Creator because they thought the great code of life had been unfairly imposed upon them.

Creator's code consisted of two laws: never take more than you need and respect your relatives.

Now these people knew that failure to live by these laws would be harmful to all other nations. They also knew that Creator would not be pleased if any part of Turtle Island suffered because the code of life had been violated. So they tried to hide their behavior from Creator.

But Coyote sat on his high hill where he was able to see everything these people did and he wondered at the deceptive conduct of the pathetic nation.

"How can they be so ignorant?" he thought. "How can they believe that Creator does not see what they are doing?"

Coyote found these people entertaining. He laughed at them, because they were always glancing sideways over their shoulders to see if they were being watched.

One day Coyote went to speak to these strange people. He sat at the edge of their village and waited for someone to acknowledge him. The few people who saw him sitting there turned away quickly because they thought if they ignored him, he'd leave.

At last a small child, too young for fear, came right up to Coyote. "Who are you?" asked the little one.

"I am your friend," said Coyote in a gentle voice.

Several other children approached him and soon the adults began to come near.

"Greetings, my friends," Coyote called. "Have no fear."

One of the men asked timidly, "Are you a spy? Were you sent by Creator to report our conduct?"

"Oh, no," Coyote chuckled. "I'm far too ordinary for such important work."

Then Coyote complained loudly about Creator's great code of life and how difficult it had made all his days.

Naturally the people agreed with Coyote and began to explain why they had grown suspicious, nervous and full of fear.

"We have decided not to live by Creator's code of life," one of them declared.

"But we are afraid we will be discovered doing something that violates those laws," someone else said.

Coyote closed his eyes and appeared to listen respectfully. From time to time he nodded his head in a solemn manner.

But he was really delighted because he knew that these fearful people were also fools. So he decided to have some fun at their expense and he opened his bag of tricks.

Coyote sat tall on his hindquarters and puffed himself up with importance. Then he cleared his throat several times and the people waited quietly for him to speak.

"I know how you can rid yourselves of your fear of Creator," he announced at last.

"How? How?' the excited people cried.

"Elect the people you want to govern you, and create your own code of life. Then appoint others to enforce the new rules. Reward those who follow the rules and punish those who do not."

Then Coyote yawned, shook his bushy tail and trotted off to his hill to see what would happen to this foolish nation.

"What a wonderful idea!" said the man who most frequently violated Creator's great code of life.

This man saw an opportunity to be important. He wanted to make laws and assign punishment. The rest of the people wanted to feel important too. The more important they felt, the less important Creator seemed to be.

Immediately they nominated and elected several people to govern and begin the task of making rules. The elected officials were instructed to make lots of rules because the more rules the people had, the safer they felt.

Of course, they stopped following Creator's good laws. In fact, they pretended that those laws no longer existed.

But, oh, how they loved their own rules!

There were rules designating who could walk which paths through the forest. There were rules concerning who, when, where and what certain people could hunt. There were rules about when and where one could gather wood. There were even rules concerning when and how one should honor Creator!

Soon the rule-makers began collecting fees and issuing permits that entitled certain people to use certain paths a specific number of times before renewing their permits. Hunting and gathering rights also had to be paid for.

Coyote laughed at the foolish people and their arrogant leaders. He laughed because now they were paying each other for the things Creator had freely given to be used by all for the welfare of all.

Those who governed became powerful and wealthy, so they appointed officials to establish tax codes and others to collect the taxes.

The government grew even more cumbersome and created new laws daily. Soon more officials were needed to enforce the abundance of laws, creating a law enforcement industry.

Those who could not pay were confined and guarded. This created yet another industry which added to the tax burden.

They had created a hungry government, a government that ate up resources, destroyed communities, and robbed people of their dignity.

Today the deluded nation continues to serve their debauched government. Many still believe the illusion that their laws make them superior and keep them safe.

Those few individuals who know they are living an illusion try to face Creator with honor. But they are penalized for their respectful conduct.

Coyote is still watching and laughing at the great joke he played on the foolish nation. For the pathetic people are in bondage to a lesser code and have burdened themselves with many unnecessary laws, when Creator gave but two.

$\mathcal{A}$ Broken Friendship

CAT AND MOUSE were once the best of friends. They enjoyed each other's company.

They were such excellent companions that Cat suggested, "We should live together. We can live quite comfortably in my big house, and we can use your small house to store our food."

So Mouse moved into Cat's house and they spent the summer and fall gathering food and getting to know each other better.

Cold Maker came with snow and wind, and winter fell upon the forest. But Cat and Mouse had no worry, for they had plenty of food stored at Mouse's house.

Then it happened that Mouse was invited to a naming ceremony.

"One of my relatives has had a child," Mouse told Cat. "They want me to come and give the child a name. It's an honor that I cannot refuse."

So he went away. He was gone for three days.

When he returned, Cat asked, "Did you have a good time?"

"Oh, my! I certainly did!"

"What did you do?"

"Oh, we sang and danced. We ate and drank. We told stories and I named that baby, too."

"What did you name the baby?"

"Ada Little Bit."

"Oh," said Cat, "that's a really cute name for a little one."

Then it happened that Mouse was invited to another naming ceremony.

Cat said, "I get kind of lonely around here. I never get to go to naming ceremonies. Do you think I could go along with you this time?"

"Oh, no!" Mouse said, "Some of my friends and relatives are afraid of you."

Cat was shocked, "But I do no harm!"

"Well, you're awfully big and you frighten the little ones."

"Tell them that I am kind and gentle."

"Yes," Mouse promised, "I'll do that."

Then he left.

After three sleeps, he returned looking plump and happy.

"Did you have a good time?" Cat asked.

"Yes! We danced, sang, ate, drank, told stories and I named the baby."

"What did you name the baby this time?"

"Ada Little More."

Cat thought friend Mouse didn't have much imagination because he'd named both babies "Ada." But he didn't say anything, as he didn't want to hurt his little friend's feelings.

Then Mouse was invited to another naming ceremony.

"Did you ask if I could come, too?" Cat wanted to know.

"Yes, I did. But no one wanted you to come. They all feel that you're just too dangerous and that you might hurt someone."

"But did you tell them that I am kind and gentle?"

"Of course, but they didn't believe me."

So mouse left.

Now Cat began to suspect that his little friend was up to something.

So when Mouse returned and Cat noticed that he was plumper than ever, he asked, "What did you name the baby this time?"

Mouse fell down laughing. "This time I named the baby 'Ate It All Up'!"

Now Cat knew that Mouse had eaten their entire food supply.

"That was a terrible thing for you to do!" Cat said. "That was food we gathered together. That was food we were going to share!

"You're selfish, greedy and dishonest! I don't want to be your friend anymore!"

Then Cat picked up Mouse and threw him far out into the snow.

To this day, Cat and Mouse are not friends, and whenever Cat finds a mouse, he eats it because he still remembers how Mouse cheated him out of his share of their winter food supply.

Courage

SONNY LIVED with his mother in a two-room shack on the edge of a swamp in northern Minnesota. The ten-year-old boy was a slow learner with poor social skills and school was often difficult for him.

Gert, his mother, had raised him on homegrown vegetables, wild fruit, venison, rabbit, partridge, US government surplus commodities and peanut butter cookies.

On a late-summer Friday in 1972 she'd been out picking blueberries most of the morning and was canning the last of them as she waited for Sonny to return from school.

She'd recently purchased a small second-hand gas range. Public Health Service had installed an electric pump in the well, a drain field and septic tank. Now they had inside plumbing complete with two sinks, a bathtub and toilet. Gert was making payments on a second-hand Maytag washing machine. These improvements had added leisure to her days and she spent much of her new found time reading.

But now she stood in the hot, steamy house canning the berries that would feed her and Sonny through the long months of winter. She wore a pair of baggy cut-off jeans and a loose white shirt. The shirt was stained with juice from several canning seasons and the seat of her pants were patched with fabric from the legs that had been cut off when the knees had worn through.

Her round face was dominated by a large nose and a broad mouth, graced by gentle eyes and transformed by a pretty smile. She smiled now as she admired the sparkle of ten mason jars filled with the bright beauty of summer fruit. But she scowled when she glanced at her nearly new electric clock. It was 4 p.m.

Quickly she stepped around the small table and looked out the window.

"Where is that boy?" she muttered. "He must have gotten off the school bus and gone right into the swamp. What's he find down there that's better than spending time with his own sweet Mama?"

She shook her head and felt her long thick braid roll across her back. Then she stirred up a bowl of pancake batter. It was almost dark when Sonny burst into the house holding his hands behind his back.

He kicked off his muddy sneakers and shouted, "Hey, Mama! Have I got something for you!"

"It's not a snake—is it?"

"Oh, Mama! You think I'm crazy? If I brought a snake in here you'd break the broom across my back."

"Well, is it a bunny?"

"It's something that doesn't need food."

"A stone?"

"Something that keeps the flies out of the kitchen."

"Daisies!"

"That's right!" The boy shouted as he whipped the flowers forward and presented them to his mother with a sweeping theatrical bow.

She smiled, took the flowers, held the boy close with one arm and prayed into his dark hair. "Oh, Creator, bless this dearest boy."

Gert recognized the value of an education and knew Sonny had problems in school. She often worried about him. "So small and thin," she thought. "So friendless and insecure."

But she pushed him away and held him at arms length for close appraisal. Then she ordered in her most impatient military voice. "Wash! And brush the spiders out of your hair."

He turned abruptly and marched into the bathroom. When she heard water running behind the flimsy door, she went into the kitchen, put the flowers in a jar of water and began making a stack of blueberry pancakes.

Sonny emerged bright-eyed and sweet smelling. He sat down, put his elbows on the table and watched his mother closely.

"Mama," he said at last. "That's real nice soap you got. Smells awful good. But could we get some of the green kind? The pink stuff makes me smell like a girl."

"That's right," she replied as she placed a plate of pancakes in front of him. "We'll get the green kind. Then I'll smell like a man."

"Oh, Mama! We could get one of each. Green for me... Pink for you."

"That's a good idea. Say, when did you get so smart?"

Sonny grinned as he spread the hot cakes with commodity surplus butter and poured a small amount of maple syrup over them. He cut off a crispy edge with the side of his fork and was lifting it to his mouth when Gert said, "Aren't you forgetting something?"

Slowly he returned the food to his plate, laid the fork on the table and bowed his head. "Creator, I thank you for this good food and my terrific Mama."

The boy was near the end of his second stack of cakes when Gert asked, "What were you doing in the swamp today?"

"Tripping traps."

"Who's trapping? Too early for furs."

"Someone's killing wild dogs and feral cats. Baiting the traps with raw meat."

Gert grimaced. "Oh, that's too bad."

Sonny nodded as he filled his mouth with the last bite.

"Mama," he said, raising his t-shirt to rub his belly. "Nobody cooks like you. You're probably the best cook on the reservation."

"Sure, and you're the best sweet-talker."

Then the boy got an old shoebox from under the fish box table and dumped it in the middle of his cot that stood against the wall opposite Gert's. He found a deck of cards tied with an old shoelace and returned to the table that his mother had already cleared and cleaned. It had become their Friday night custom to play gin until bedtime. Gert had taken the lead last week. But by 10 p.m. Sonny had regained his championship status.

"Time for bed!" he shouted before Gert could challenge him for a rematch.

When they got into their beds and turned off the lamp, they laid in the darkness for a long time listening to the owls calling across the swamp. Gert's elders had said that Creator designated owls as nighttime messengers. She told Sonny these birds were responsible for the most urgent revelations. They brought both good news and ill tidings. They also carried gifts.

"They bring the news that cannot wait for day," she told him.

Now the boy listened prayerfully to the messages the owls were carrying through the dark sky.

The next morning Gert got up to find that Sonny had already gone. "Oh, that little swamp rat," she grumbled.

But she smiled as she made a pot of coffee and hummed as she wondered what she should do with this bright Saturday morning Creator had provided for her and her son. When she sat down to enjoy the cup of hot brew, she saw Sonny hurrying toward the house. He was carrying something wrapped in his olive-drab jacket. She ran out to meet him.

"It's an owl!" he screamed. "He was caught in a trap! He can't fly! Oh, Mama, you've got to help him!"

"Dear God," Gert moaned.

He carried the owl into the house and laid it on the table.

She opened the jacket and winced. The owl's right foot was crushed and torn. But although his feathers were bent and battered, his wings were not broken. The emaciated bird was nearly comatose.

"He'll need raw meat," Gert said as she took a dollar from her handbag. "You must ride to town and buy some hamburger."

Sonny snatched the bill from her fingers, dashed out of the house and ran to the shed where he kept his old bike. She watched him pedal furiously down the road and out of sight. Then she turned her attention to the injured owl.

Gently she gathered him in her arms, carried him to the bathroom and laid him in the gleaming white tub. Then she prepared a pan of warm water, added a small amount of hydrogen peroxide and cleaned the mangled foot. The owl didn't move.

When Sonny returned he spread his jacket in the tub and placed a bit of hamburger and a bowl of water near the owl's head. He watched his mother dip a small amount of meat into the water and offer it to the four directions. Then she held the owl upright in her arms, pressed the meat into his hooked beak and waited for him to swallow. Then she repeated the process three more times.

The boy wept as he stroked the soft breast feathers of the helpless owl and thought of how he'd struggled alone through several fearful days and painful nights. At last the boy had understood the owl's call and went to find him.

"His name is Courage," he said.

The owl accepted the tub as his nest and his mess making was confined to that area. They covered one end of the tub with boards to provide a small dark place for the owl to sleep. Sonny improved the nest with twigs, leaves and pine needles. Gert provided a box of dry sand and Courage took dust baths once or twice a day.

During the following weeks Gert and Sonny could not use their new tub. So they resumed bathing in the old galvanized bathtub that had enjoyed a brief period of retirement when the government brought indoor plumbing to their small house.

To Courage's diet of raw hamburger Sonny added perch, frogs, salamanders and an occasional mouse. The owl maneuvered the food around until it could be swallowed whole. Whatever the owl couldn't digest was ejected orally in mucus-thickened pellets during the night. Sonny examined the pellets in the morning and collected the small bones.

Gert made Sonny a small leather bag which he wore around his neck when he was not in school. He put seven Courage-bones in the bag. The rest of the bones went into a tobacco can that he kept under his bed. Sonny spent most of his time with Courage and in a short time he became proficient at imitating the owl's rather large vocabulary. Although she didn't imitate the owl, Gert enjoyed talking to Courage. The owl turned his face toward her as she spoke, giving her his complete attention. He looked out at her from bright, thoughtful eyes and seemed to understand.

Eventually Courage grew so fond of the woman he would sit on her shoulder and gently groom her hair with his fierce looking beak. So they nurtured one another until, on a frosty November morning it was time for Courage to leave.

Gert carried him outside and set him on a low limb in a young white pine. He sat there for a long time. Then he flew out of the pine tree to a nearby maple and perched above them, looking down on the boy and his mother. At last he rose high on his silent wings, circled several times and turned west. They watched him disappear into the distant gray sky. Then they stood staring into that place long after he'd vanished from view.

For several days they grieved in the vacuum Courage left. They missed his hooting and cackling, and dancing in the tub. The tiny bathroom, where he'd sat on the sink to preen his feathers or stare out of the small window, seemed large and cold without him. Meanwhile, Sonny would almost see Courage perched on the edge of the tub exercising his short, full wings. When he bathed, it seemed that Courage was nearby. He looked at the Courage-bones again and again.

Then in December Sonny began to enjoy the companionship of his first school friend. Oscar Whidbey was small for his age and walked with a slight limp. He'd moved to Bena with his parents, three dogs and a cat. He told Sonny that he used to have a turtle and a toad. But he'd left them in Michigan. Sonny liked him as soon as he saw him. He told Gert that Oscar was his third best friend.

"You're still number one," he explained. "Then there's Courage and then Oscar."

One day Oscar came home with Sonny after school and Gert was surprised at how familiar the child seemed. "Something about his eyes," she thought. "So large and bright."

Later that day Oscar's mother came to get him in an old yellow pick-up. Gert was out at the mailbox when the woman arrived, opened the truck door and leaped lightly to the ground. She shook her shoulders, tossed her blond hair, kicked at the snow with her narrow boot, extended her thin hand and said, "Hello, Gert. I'm Nellie Whidbey."

The women walked to the house together. Sonny pulled two red folding chairs from under his cot and they all crowded around the table as Gert poured two cups of coffee and two glasses of milk. Then she set out a plate of commodity surplus peanut butter cookies.

"I hope my boy wasn't a bother," Nellie said as she rubbed Oscar on the head with the tips of her long fingers. "Sometimes he gets real nosy and wants to know everything at once. I told him some people don't like little boys who ask a lot of questions. If he gets on your nerves you tell him to keep quiet."

They both smiled at Gert, looking out at her with their large bright eyes.

The next time Oscar came to visit, Sonny took him into the swamp and showed him where he'd found Courage. Hissing mournfully, Oscar squatted down and held his right foot. Then he flapped his arms and tumbled about in the snow while Sonny wept. At last Sonny pulled Oscar to his feet, brushed the snow off his jacket and led him back to the house.

Gert had prepared a macaroni hot-dish with onions and ground venison. When the boys came in she set three chipped, mismatched plates on the table. The boys hung up their jackets, washed their hands and sat down to eat.

"You like owls, don't you?" Oscar asked softly as he spooned a large serving of the hot-dish onto his plate. Sonny had already filled his mouth and could not speak, but he nodded emphatically.

"Yes, I do," Gert said. "I like almost everything around here." Leaning forward, she added quietly, "I especially like little boys."

Oscar slipped off he chair and stepping around the table, wrapped his thin arms around Gert's neck. The woman held the child for a long time. Something about that small warm body just wouldn't let her go.

When Nellie came for her boy, she told Gert that they were leaving Bena. "My husband got work in Washington State."

"Logging?" Gert asked.

"Heavens no!" the woman gasped.

Before Oscar rode off with his mother that day, the boys exchanged gifts and promises.

"What did you give him?" Gert asked.

"My Swiss army knife."

"Oh, Sonny," she whispered. "That was Uncle Steve's old knife. I know how you loved it."

She held her son close for a long time. Then she asked, "What did you promise?"

"Oh, Mama! You know I can't tell you. It's a secret."

"Well, what did he give you?"

He went to the cot and returned with the shoebox and removed the lid. Lying on top of all his treasures was a pale feather with a fluted edge.

"A feather," he told her. "An owl feather."

As she watched the boy stroke the feather with his fingertip, she bit her lip and fought back her tears as she prayed. "Oh, Creator, bless my lonely-again-boy."

Soon after that, school became a pleasant distraction for the child. The teacher introduced his students to birds of prey with a particular emphasis on the barred owl. Sonny had learned a lot from Courage and soon he was the undisputed classroom expert. He surpassed the instructor in his knowledge of owl behavior and amazed everyone with owl calls.

One day Sonny asked Gert to go with him to the place where he'd found Courage. "I want to bury the old bones now," he told her.

As she followed him through the swamp, Gert was surprised at how tall he'd grown. How broad his shoulders had become. Then she watched him dig a shallow hole. He lined the hole with cedar and laid the bone bag on the green bed. Afterwards he sprinkled it with tobacco and prayed. Carefully he returned the soil, pressed it down with his hand and covered it with a red agate.

Although Sonny soon had other friends, his memories of Courage and Oscar were kept alive by owls that arrived with messages from the West. He often found their fringed feathers on the sill of the bathroom window. Sometimes he stared into the glass pane and saw Courage and Oscar looking back.

Gert saw them. Too.

Winter Thunder

IT HAPPENED one day that old Maggie Jigs was gathering wood along an ice-locked river, when she was surprised to hear the distant rumble of winter thunder followed by hoarse squawks of a great blue heron.

"How can this be?" she wondered. "Heron cannot hunt food in ice covered waters. Therefore, he cannot survive in the cold winter. Surely I do not hear the call of Heron. Surely I am mistaken."

She pulled the fringed hood of her brown capote closer around her neck and quickly made her way to the place where the sound was coming from.

Once more she was surprised. Although she saw no heron, there in the snow stood a large feather, and it was certainly the feather of the great blue heron.

Slowly she removed a fur-lined deerskin mitten, bent over and picked up the tall blue-grey feather. For several minutes she considered the remote possibility that a heron had somehow failed to fly south for the winter. But where would he find food? In the end it seemed quite unlikely. So she stuck the feather in her hair, put on her mitten and went on gathering wood.

Before going very far, she was startled by the melodious whistle of a bluebird.

"How can this be?" she wondered once again. "Bluebird cannot find flying insects in winter and, therefore, cannot survive the cold. Surely I do not hear the song of Bluebird. Surely I am mistaken."

Then she made her way to the place where the song had come from and found a tiny feather standing in the snow. Indeed it was the feather of Bluebird.

She picked up the delicate pale blue feather, stuck it in her hair and went on gathering wood.

Once more she was stopped by the call of a bird. This time she heard Killdeer, repeating its name again and again.

"How can this be?" she thought. "Surely Killdeer can find no food in the winter and survive such cold."

But she went to the place where the song was coming from and found a feather standing in the snow. It was, of course, Killdeer's feather.

Carefully she picked up the orange tail feather, stuck it in her hair and went on gathering wood.

When she heard the scream of the Red-Tailed Hawk, she was not surprised. But she put down her bundle of wood, went to the place where the sound came from and found a feather standing in the snow. Yes, it was the feather of a Red-Tailed Hawk. She stuck the banded wing feather in her hair and waited.

At this point she realized that she was getting closer to the small log house she shared with her old man. When she'd left to gather wood, he'd been sleeping like a bear. She wondered if he was awake now, and if he'd put more wood in the stove or let the fire die. She hoped he'd made a pot of corn meal mush.

Suddenly she heard the coo of a Mourning Dove, followed by the whistling of wings.

She went to the place where the sounds had come from and found a long sharp feather of a Mourning Dove standing in the snow. She stuck the feather in her hair and waited.

Not far away she heard the spring song of a Robin calling for rain. She hurried to the place and found a dark feather from Robin standing in the snow. She tucked it into her hair and waited again.

Then she heard the flute-like song of the Meadowlark.

She went to the place where the sound came from and found a small, banded tail feather standing in the snow. It was Meadowlark's feather. She stuck that in her hair, too.

Maggie stood quite still and listened carefully for the song of another bird, but except for the wind in the treetops, the forest had become very quiet.

Then she heard the slight crunch of snow under a furtive step. She looked back and saw a pack of wild dogs moving toward her.

Clearly she was being stalked.

It was a long way for an old woman to run but she started hurrying toward home. The dogs moved quickly in her direction.

Maggie knew that wild dogs often attacked people in winter. While wolves feared people and ran from them, wild dogs had no such fears. Remembering their old man-inflicted injuries, wild dogs become mad with hate and tear their victims bloody. If the victim dies, the dogs return later to feast on human flesh.

Her heart was pounding and pain filled her bony chest as she stumbled along. Then she heard someone shout, "Get down!"

She sprawled on the snow and covered her ears as several bullets whistled over her head.

Then someone was gently shaking her shoulder. "Are you all right?" asked her anxious husband as he lifted her to her feet and held her close.

"Yes, yes," she gasped. "But how did you know?"

"I was awakened by winter thunder," he said. "I was worried about you. So I got the gun and started following your tracks. But soon I was distracted by strange bird songs. Songs I'd never heard in winter. So I followed the songs instead. As I went along I gathered these feathers."

She looked up and saw seven feathers stuck in his tousled white hair.

As they stood staring at each other in amazement, Raven dropped out of the sky and sat near them.

Raven made the calls of Heron, Bluebird, Killdeer, Mourning Dove, Hawk, Robin and Meadowlark. Then hopping upward, Raven opened his great wings, circled the old couple seven times and flew away filling the sky with winter thunder.

That night the grateful old man made a long narrow cedar box for the feathers. Maggie cut a birch bark pattern of Raven and her old man carved it into the lid.

During the years that followed, Maggie often told visitors how Raven had led her away from the wild dogs by imitating several birds and leaving their feathers in the snow.

Then she'd open the small cedar box and lay seven feathers before the astonished listeners.

Her old man would tell how Raven had led him to Maggie. Then he'd take seven more feathers from the box to prove that it was so.

When the elders passed on, the feathers disappeared from the closed box. Then, several years later, the box burned in a house fire. All that remains is this story.

Fights the Bear

WHEN MY GREAT-UNCLE George came home from the army after World War II, he was in good physical shape and conditioned for fighting. He was no bully but he enjoyed an opportunity to demonstrate his self-defense skills and flex his well-earned muscles. So when a carnival came to the Red Lake Reservation with a black bear who wrestled men, George felt confident that he could stay in the ring with that bear for at least one minute.

He watched the bear move and saw how he tumbled men around for about half a minute before picking them up and tossing them out of the ring. When he thought he knew the bear's strategy, he paid the five-dollar bet against the bear and got into the ring.

At first the bear seemed puzzled by the big Indian man who stalked him and boxed him. It soon appeared that the bear had met his match. But before the bell rang, George was flung out of the ring and lost his five dollars.

The man who ran the show slapped George on the back and said, "You almost had him! A few more seconds and you would have won. I think you should take another chance. This time I'll hypnotize the bear so he'll be afraid of you. I know you can win then."

George was suspicious and asked the man why he'd want his bear to lose.

The man replied, "It's good for business if the customer wins once in a while."

It made sense. So George paid another five dollars and watched as the man hypnotized his bear. Soon they were in the ring again.

The bear ran around and around the ring trying to escape. The crowd cheered and began placing bets on George. Now George was an extremely strong man and when he caught the bear he wrapped his powerful arms around him. He held him tight and began dragging him toward the ropes. The bear cried like a baby and tried to squirm free, but George held on.

The crowd was screaming as the clock hand approached the one-minute mark. Suddenly the bear pulled himself free, picked George up and flung him out of the ring again. All the wind went out of the audience as the owner of the bear collected on the bets.

When I was a child, Uncle George always made me laugh when he told this story.

"But," he'd say, "that man must have hypnotized me by mistake, because from that day I've always been afraid to fight with bears."

Agatha's Secret

A GATHA ROSE had a secret.

No one would guess that the slender girl with large flat feet was anyone special. But she possessed a potent power that few enjoy today.

She'd discovered it quite by accident when she was fifteen years old. It was in early spring when morels were lifting their dark heads above the forest floor. She was, in fact, hunting the flavorful mushrooms.

It was that lovely time of year before mosquito larvae matured.

With her small basket she walked in silence. Her shoulders were slightly hunched as she stepped carefully across the mottled brown mat of last year's fallen leaves.

Suddenly she froze and from the corners of both eyes she saw deer at her left and right. In that instant three distant stars converged in perfect alignment with Agatha and she was transformed. She had become a shape-shifter.

Her basket fell and her morels tumbled out. Then on shining black hooves she stepped over the basket and went on foraging. Occasionally a vagrant deer fly buzzed her ears. It was annoying, but not unbearable.

The other deer were startled, but soon accepted her as one of them. They spent the rest of the day munching morels together.

As the sky lost its brilliant blue, Agatha began to change. Soon she was a girl again. It was a stunning moment!

She found herself naked and alone in the growing darkness. She hurried back to where she'd transformed. It didn't take her long to find her basket, her clothes and her shoes.

But because she was such a young shape-shifter, she had returned to herself with deer teeth. She found them very uncomfortable.

Her mother was mildly surprised when Agatha came home with an empty basket. The distraught girl picked up a magazine, covered her mouth and said haltingly, "I... had a basket... of morels... but... I ate... them."

"Agatha should see the dentist," her father commented at the supper table. "Her teeth interfere with her speech."

So, the next morning Mother called the Indian Health Service clinic to make an appointment. The dentist, however, was overbooked and could not see Agatha for six months.

The following week found her transformed into a skunk. She ambled down the muddy road on a rainy night. She held her tail over her back to shed water. She loved the squishiness around her feet.

Suddenly a very small skunk burst from the underbrush and approached her. They stood nose to nose and neither was offended by the odor of the other.

Still, she had not mastered the art of shape shifting and returned to herself with a streak of white down the middle of her head. She hid in the outhouse until she got her hair back to normal.

Once she shifted into a robin, ate several rosy worms but found she was unable to fly. No matter how she flapped her wings and jumped about, she could not rise. For this she would need expert instruction.

Agatha returned to herself with a single row of dark feathers around her eyes. She thought they were quite attractive and enjoyed them for several splendid days.

Mother thought Agatha was using mascara and Father didn't notice.

Then she jumped into a nearby lake and shifted into a large mouth bass. It was a glorious experience! But after several exciting hours of dipping, diving and leaping from the water to snatch darting dragonflies out of the sky, she retuned to herself and went home.

That night she discovered silver scales on her shoulders and down the back of both arms. She washed with vinegar and went to bed. In the morning the scales were gone.

On another occasion she changed into a soft gray mole and dug a perfect home in the dark shallow earth. She lined it with rose petals and welcomed four fabulous beetles to join her for a lovely housewarming party. The beetles sang wonderful songs! She told fantastic stories.

Agatha became a private young woman who didn't make friends easily. She always felt that her secret ability might be unacceptable to others, and so didn't share it with anyone.

But one day a fine young man decided to marry Agatha. He professed his deep love, proposed his intentions and claimed her hand.

"I can teach you to fly," he promised.

Then it happened while they were swimming in a moonlit river, fragrant with white water lilies, that Agatha transformed into an otter. To her delight, he transformed into an otter, too.

He was also an expert aviator and flying instructor. Soon Agatha could fly with robins, hummingbirds and eagles. They spent the winter in Mexico and often shape shifted into monkeys, butterflies and parrots.

And they lived happily ever after.

Horse Trade

BILLY BOWLEGS greatly admired Martin Van Pelt's new wagon and team of horses. The big red-brown mares were a near match. Both had long black tails and clipped black manes. They had bright white diamonds in the middle of their long handsome faces.

"Mighty fine outfit," Billy said to himself.

Martin thought he recognized the longing look of envy in Billy's eyes and he smiled. Then he gave the horses a smart slap on their rumps with the loose reins. Immediately they lifted their feet higher and moved more quickly down the road. Martin tipped his hat toward the Indian as he passed.

But Billy paid no attention to the farmer. Instead he imagined himself sitting up on the wagon coaxing the team along toward the small house he shared with his wife, her sister, her nephew and an elderly uncle.

Although the horses were both mares, Martin called them Prince Albert and Queen Victoria. He enjoyed the small feeling of power it gave him when he slapped the royal pair to a quicker pace.

"I'd rename them," Billy told himself. "One would be Agnes, for my wife. The other would be Amik, for my mother."

It was a long road, and as he went Billy thought of his tired family walking to town. He thought of his wife walking home, her back strained under a heavy bag of flour. Then he thought of her sitting beside him on the wagon bench with their family riding behind in the box. He saw his uncle sitting on a bag of flour laughing.

"Billy, Billy," he heard the old man say.

When he got home, Billy went to the barn where his uncle was mending a broken rope.

"Uncle White Horse," Billy said, "I heard you calling."

"Yes," he replied. "I have had a vision. Creator wants to help us. At the same time we will be teaching old Van Pelt a good lesson. Perhaps that man will become a human being at last."

The next time Martin passed the Bowlegs' place he saw a magnificent white stallion standing near the fence.

"Good God!" Martin exclaimed. "Where did that no-account Indian get such a beautiful horse? He must have stolen it!"

"No," the sheriff told him later that day. "No reports of stolen horses in the area."

Then Martin asked everyone he met if they knew where Billy Bowlegs had bought the new horse. No one had seen it before. Its origin was a mystery.

Martin couldn't sleep.

"It's not fair," he thought. "That worthless Indian shouldn't own such a fine looking animal. It should be mine. But how can I get it from him?"

That night Billy dreamed that one of the mares had thrown a shoe. So the next morning he got up early, tied two bundles of tobacco, put on his old leather gloves and rode over to Martin's on the white stallion.

"Billy," the wealthy farmer said, "one of my mares threw a shoe. I'll give you a dollar to fix her up for me."

So Billy tied the stallion to a fence post and went into the warm barn. He stood several minutes as his eyes became adjusted to the shadows.

Martin watched the Indian disappear into the dark yawn of the barn door before approaching the white horse.

"My God!" the farmer prayed, "this is the kind of a horse I've always wanted. That Indian has no right to own such a fine creature. I've got to have this horse. Amen."

After Billy had soothed and shod the mare, he dug a small hole in the earthen floor of both stalls and buried a glove in each hole. Then he hung the tobacco bundles up in the rafters where no one would find them and went home to wait.

It wasn't long before Martin was at Billy's door. He'd brought his foreman and two other men.

"Billy," the farmer beamed. "I want to buy your horse."

"No," Billy answered. "I can't sell him. I need him."

Agnes, her sister and the boy gathered close and listened.

"Tell me what you paid for him," Martin insisted. "I'll double it."

"I don't need money," Billy said. "I need a horse."

"All right. I'll trade both my mares for your stallion," the farmer bargained.

"Well, I don't know," Billy considered. "That's the best horse I've ever had."

"I'll throw in the wagon, too."

Then Billy smiled, extended his right hand and said, "It's a deal."

So the trade was made and Martin rode home on the big white horse. For several days he paraded the horse all over the county, bragging about how he got the best of Billy Bowlegs. But one day he went to the barn, found the doors open and the horse gone.

"That Indian has stolen my horse!" he yelled. The rafters shook, the spiders scrambled and two small bundles of tobacco trembled. Quickly Martin rode over to Billy's with his foreman.

"You stole my horse!" he accused.

"I did no such thing," Billy said.

"Well, he's gone! Now I want my wagon and those mares back!"

The foreman was surprised. He urged Martin to remember that there had been several witnesses to the horse trade.

"You can't take my wagon and horses," Billy said. "It's not my fault that he's gone."

"We'll look for him," the foreman promised as he led his shaken boss away. "He can't have wandered far."

So Martin and the foreman looked for the white stallion for several days. At last they gave up the search and returned to running the large prosperous farm.

Fortunately Martin had waited until the trail was cold before looking for the horse. If he'd been quicker he'd have seen how the stallion's tracks had suddenly became man tracks. He would have followed those tracks to Billy's barn where he'd have found Uncle White Horse mending a rope.

Now whenever Billy and his family pass Martin's place, the farmer seethes with jealousy as he watches them go happily along their way in the wagon that had once belonged to him being pulled by two fine mares that were once his own.

When Billy sees Martin watching, he slaps the mares lightly with the loose reins.

"Get along Agnes, Get along Amik," he calls softly.

Oh, they pull up their heads, lift their feet high and prance proudly toward the small farm they share with Billy and his family.

It's in the Corn

IT WAS THANKSGIVING DAY again and I was preparing to drive to the Leech Lake Reservation to visit my son and his family. It was a five-hour drive so I wanted to get an early start. But as I reached the door, the phone rang. It was my old friend Angeline. She told me of an unusual incident that had occurred on her farm the previous day.

After putting out organic corn to feed the deer who lived in her beautiful woodland refuge, she'd gone inside to look for warmer socks. As she opened and closed the bureau drawers she'd become aware of a peculiar tension and looking up found that several familiar deer had posted themselves near the windows. Upon closer examination she realized that some of the deer in the yard were strangers to her.

"I had the distinct impression that my deer friends were protecting me from the newcomers," she told me.

The deer had maintained their posts for about 30 minutes and then the newcomers left. The resident deer ate their corn but milled about the yard for another hour before disappearing into the forest.

I considered Angeline's strange story as I drove the long road to Tom's house to have dinner with him, his wife and children. I was looking forward to good food and a good long visit.

Driving along Highway 200 I was struck again by the lack of birds. It had been like this for several months. It began with the arrival of a viral infection that invaded the blood of birds. Songbirds were most vulnerable. Rapidly it had spread until nearly all the singers had died.

"What kind of a day has no bird songs?" I wondered.

Then I saw something large in a tree on the left side of the road. I opened the window and slowed to a crawl. When I got close enough I realized that it was a great gray owl. He stared at me without moving. Then suddenly he leaped up, crossed the road and flew ahead of me. He landed in a dead tree and watched me approach again. As I passed, he flew to another tree about one hundred yards down the road. He repeated this strange ritual several times then flew off into the trees and I didn't see him again.

Since owls are rarely seen flying during the day, I closed the window and pulled the car onto the narrow shoulder of the road to consider the mysterious event. Then I took my tobacco pouch from my coat pocket and got out of the car to pray. I stood beside the road to thank Creator for allowing this amazing owl to survive the viral epidemic. Then, because owls carry messages from the spirit world, I asked that the wisdom the owl carried be made clear to me. Then I sprinkled tobacco on the ground and left.

A few miles down the road I saw a large gathering of deer in a low meadow. They watched me pass but didn't move. There was something ominous in their fearless stares.

When I got to Tom's I was surprised to see a great gray owl perched on the bird feeder. Then I saw that the windows on both his truck and Missy's car were shattered. As I got out of the car Tom burst out of the front door and hurried toward me. He was carrying a rifle. Quickly he ushered me up the steps and into the house.

"Where's everyone?" I asked.

"In the garage," he whispered hoarsely as he glanced nervously toward the forest.

He took my arm and propelled me hastily down the hall and into the garage where the rest of the family waited. The children were unusually quiet and Missy appeared shaken as she came forward to embrace me. After I'd hugged everyone, Tom began telling me a strange story.

"The deer are watching us. They have a leader who has become aggressive. He rushed us when we tried to leave and he attacked the vehicles."

"Call your father," I suggested. "He likes to kill deer."

"I did," Tom replied.

"What happened?"

"He told me that the deer had his house surrounded and he couldn't leave."

"Have you called the DNR?"

"Yes, but they have their hands full. Calls are coming in from all over and they are only responding to the most urgent situations. They think they will have to call in the National Guard. But for now, they feel I can protect my own family."

I looked around the garage. It was obvious that they were ready to fight. They had gathered bats, hockey sticks, golf clubs, umbrellas, shovels, rakes, guns, bows and arrows.

They had put up bunk beds, made a cooking area and curtained off a corner of the garage for privacy.

"We'll be safe in here." Tom assured us. "The deer don't seem interested in the garage, because they can't see us. I'm sure they'll try to break the windows in the house. The leader is not only fearlessly aggressive, but intelligent. The other deer are learning from him. Today he showed them how to break windows."

I was chilled by what he told me.

"I don't want to kill them if I don't have to," he said. "Maybe they'll get tired of prowling about and just go away."

I hadn't seen any deer when I arrived so I asked where they were.

"They heard the car coming and hid behind the house."

Changing the subject to relieve the tension, I asked, "Did you see the owl?

"Yes," Missy said. "He arrived yesterday... before the deer came. The owl is one of my spirit helpers. I think he came to guide us through this ordeal. I think that as long as he stays... we should stay and not try to run away."

Just then we heard heavy deer steps on the deck. We held our collective breath. Then the deer began striking the window with their hooves. Again and again they hit the glass. After a few minutes the window exploded into the room and the deer were inside the house. We could still hear deer walking on the deck so we knew that not all the deer had entered. But surely the leader had and he'd brought a couple of bold bucks with him. They milled about in the house for about ten minutes.

Then they leaped out of the broken window. Soon they were gone. But the silence they left behind was terrifying. We waited several more minutes before we dared to move or speak.

"I think if we killed the leader they might leave for awhile," Tom said. "But I'm afraid they'll return more angry and more aggressive."

"What did the DNR officers say about this?" I asked.

"Apparently they saw it coming. For years they've been receiving calls about deer breaking into cabins and attacking vehicles. They have also begun to find deer hunters trampled and dead in the woods. The information was not made public because they didn't want to start a panic. To make hunting less appealing, they began spreading rumors of mad deer disease."

"Do they know what causes the aggressive conduct?"

"They found an abnormal gene that produces highly intelligent deer. The deer population has exploded, you know. So incidents of deer attacks have increased because more of the aggressive deer are surviving."

I was astounded. "Do they know how the mutation began?"

"It's in the corn," Tom told me. "It's in the corn."

Food for Little People

ONE DAY A YOUNG BOY was traveling with his grandparents and they were caught in a terrible storm. There was wind and rain and thunder and hail. Grandfather covered the horse's head with a sack and tied the frightened animal to a tree. The family took shelter under the wagon.

Grandfather dug a shallow hole in the earth, put in a fistful of tobacco and prayed for the safety of his wife and grandson. So the storm passed without doing them any harm.

Then he said to the boy, "Go to bed and cover yourself well. We will have a strange little visitor tonight. Don't look at him."

Quickly the boy prepared for bed and the elders covered him with a blanket. They tucked it around him so tightly that he could not move. Then they pulled it up to cover his head. Afterwards they covered themselves, too.

But the boy found he was able to peek out through a small hole in the blanket. He lay there for a long time wondering whom his grandparents were expecting. At last the stranger stepped into view. The boy was surprised to see a tiny man with a brown wrinkled face and small bright eyes. His hair was long and uncombed. He wore a deerskin skirt wrapped around his waist. It hung to his knees. His feet and head were bare. The little man went right to where the elders were sleeping and put his hand on the woman's shoulder.

"Please," he said softly, "I would like to have some food."

Quickly the woman got up and gave him some deer meat and dried fish. But the man did not want to eat.

"Please, put the food in a bundle," he said. "I am taking it to my people."

So she wrapped the food carefully and the little man carried it away.

The next morning the boy's face was puffed up so big that he couldn't open his eyes.

His grandfather said, "I told you not to look at our visitor. Now you have been warned."

They were unable to travel because of the boy's condition so they slept in that place again. That night the little man returned and asked the woman for more food.

This time the boy didn't try to look at the visitor. But before the man left with the food, he stood near the boy and whistled softly until the boy went to sleep. In the morning he was fully recovered.

For the rest of his life the boy would hear that tiny whistle and know that little people were nearby. Then he'd put out small baskets of fish or dried berries for them to take. In the morning it would all be gone. Sometimes a small feather of friendship or a shiny stone of appreciation would be left where the basket of generosity had been.

Then it happened when the man had reached the third hill of his earth journey that he came upon the body of a little man laying on a flat rock. The well-formed body was dark and wrinkled. It was wrapped in a short deerskin skirt. Immediately he recognized the little man he'd seen in his grandparents' camp so many years before.

The man had never heard of anyone who had been permitted to witness such a thing and it frightened him to be chosen for such an honor. He did not speak of this event until he himself had grown quite old. Whenever he told this story he put a handful of tobacco down in front of him so those who heard him would know he spoke the truth.

They say when he was preparing to go over to the other side, the little people came to help him along. Although no one saw them, their tiny whistles came up out of the tall grass around the village.

Therefore, the mourners knew that many little people were present. The elders believed that all the little people the man had fed while he lived had come to encourage him as he set off upon his last journey.

Little Old Woman and the Hunters

Two brothers were walking down the road with their new guns. They were looking for targets. As they went along they spoke loudly of what they would do to any squirrels they saw.

"I'll blast their guts out!" one of them boasted.

The other sneered. "I'll rip them in half."

They laughed over the bloody fate of their defenseless little tree-climbing brothers.

Suddenly the taller boy yelled, "I see one!"

He raised his gun and fired without aiming. The squirrel disappeared. Almost immediately a dead blue jay fell on the ground before them.

"I wasn't trying to hit the squirrel," the tall boy lied. "I was aiming at that bird all along."

Then they walked on looking for more targets. Ten minutes later a curious chipmunk met his end. Not long after that a busy red squirrel bit the dust. As they walked on talking about what great hunters they were becoming they began to feel that they were being watched.

Suddenly they tripped over nothing, fell on their bellies and watched their shiny new guns bounce along the rut-road and dive into the water-filled ditch. Fear blanched their faces as they realized that they would have to explain this to their father. They climbed slowly to their feet and were surprised to see Little Old Woman standing behind them.

"Having trouble?" she asked with a chuckle and a wink.

"Nothing we can't handle," muttered the tall boy.

They got a long pole and dragged it through the muddy water hoping to pull the guns up. But that only buried them deeper in the black mud. To their surprise Little Old Woman began picking up wood and when she had enough, she built a small fire. Then, taking a pot from her bag, she began to cook.

Almost at once the boys were hungry and soon they were starving. Little Old Woman sang softly as she stirred the pot. In a few minutes she was sipping a delicious bowl of soup while the boys watched.

"Well," the tall boy complained, "we're hungry, too."

"Aren't you going to share your meal?" the small one grumbled.

"Oh," Little Old Woman replied, "I should think such great hunters would have their own soup. I saw you kill the blue jay, chipmunk and squirrel."

"Augh!" the tall boy said with a disgusted grimace. "No one eats those things."

"You eat what you kill," the woman replied.

At that moment the day darkened and turned quickly into night. The two boys moved closer to Little Old Woman's fire.

"What pitiful hunters you are," she told them as she poured each of them a bowl of hot soup. After they had eaten they lay down and went to sleep.

In the morning they awakened to find the shiny guns standing against a nearby tree. They took the guns and without speaking went to find the dead squirrel, chipmunk and blue jay. Without boasting they carried them to Little Old Woman's house. She threw open the door before they knocked. Immediately she offered a prayer of thanksgiving for the spirits of those who died so two hungry boys could eat.

Later she cleaned and washed the blue jay. She salted the wings, spread them on a board and nailed them down to dry. She pulled the skins off the chipmunk and squirrel, washed and salted the small hides and stretched them over two boards with the fury sides inward. She hung them from the rafters.

Then she told the boys to build a small fire and get a kettle of water. She skewered the bird to a long green stick. Then the small boy held it over the fire while the other wrapped the squirrel in basswood leaves and buried it under the coals. The chipmunk was cut into small pieces and boiled in the pot. Little Old Woman added some wild onions and a bit of rice. Soon they were ready to eat.

It has been said that these two boys became the most respected hunters on the Leech Lake Reservation.

The Coin

IT WAS THE WINTER of 1945 and twelve year old Billy Whitefeather
had been working for Mary Kingbird all week. Yesterday she'd promised,
"When you finish the job, I'll pay you for the work you've done."

Now, Billy flogged himself with his long arms and stamped his feet as he
waited for Mary to answer his knock. The December cold pressed through his
worn jacket. He pulled his cap down closer around his ears. He cupped his
hands over his mouth and blew some warmth into his ragged mittens. Then
he folded his arms across his chest and tucked his hands into his armpits. He
turned to study the neatly stacked pile of split wood near the back of the house.
"It will last for several weeks," he thought.

He remembered the sweat and toil, the heavy ax raised again and again,
the long hours walking home alone in the cold darkness. He'd felt he'd been
measured and proven. Then the door opened, and Billy turned to find Mary
looking at him. "Are you finished?' she asked.

Billy nodded. Mary leaned out and peered toward the woodpile. She
slipped her arthritic fingers painfully into a small beaded purse hanging from
her belt. Then her hand emerged and pressed a coin into Billy's mitten.

"Miigwech," he said as he backed away from the door. He turned and
quickly stepped off the sagging porch.

Billy did not look at the coin as he trudged along the trail from Mary's tired-looking house. He held it tightly while a lump thickened in his aching throat. "Oh," he moaned toward a watchful chickadee, "she only gave me a quarter!" How terribly disappointed he was. "But," he consoled himself, "Twenty-five cents, added to the seventy-five cents I already have, will still buy a good gift for Mother."

He hurried down the hill. When he was sure that Mary could no longer see him, he stopped to put the coin in his pocket. Tears filled his eyes as he stared in disbelief at the shiny nickel. He let the coin slide off his mitten and watched it roll down the trail a short distance. "She cheated me!" he hissed between clenched teeth.

He wanted to return to Mary's house, to push the woodpile over and throw the wood out into the brush. But he wanted to obey his mother, too. "Billy," she'd told him many times, "always treat your elders with respect."

Late the next day, Mary arrived at Billy's house carrying a bundle under her arm.

Billy's mother quickly placed a chair near the wood stove and the old woman sat down. Mother brought a cup of maple-sweetened tea to the visitor. After she'd sipped at the hot tea for several minutes, Mary said, "I have something for Billy."

She handed the package to him. "Open it," she urged. Her soft voice carried her kindness and her eyes were full of pleasure. "You did a good job for me, but you worked too quickly," she told him. "You finished your work for me before I had finished my work for you."

Carefully Billy laid the package on the table. Slowly he opened it. Inside was a pair of beaded deerskin mittens.

"Put them on," coaxed Mary.

The smoky smell of newly tanned hide filled the room. Billy pushed his hand into the soft rabbit fur lining. The mink-trimmed cuff reached half way up to his elbow.

They were the finest mittens Billy had ever seen. He stared at the intricate floral designs and thought of Mary's small, aching fingers holding the fine beading needle. He thought of her tired eyes finding the tiny holes in each bead. He thought of the woodpile still standing in neat stacks near her house.

"Miigwech, Grandmother," he whispered.

Mary smiled.

When she was ready to leave, Billy put on his jacket, cap and new mittens. "I'll walk with you," he said, offering her his strong arm.

Billy's mother watched them walk slowly down the trail in the gathering darkness. Then she turned from the steamy window to set the table for supper. She thought of the shiny nickel she'd found on the trail that morning. She took the coin from her pocket and slid it under Billy's plate.

A Perfect Gift

THE FROZEN GROUND sounded hollow under Willy's heavy boots. After every few steps he would turn back to look toward the sleeping village. The little cluster of houses seemed so far away. He knew that soon he would not be able to see them at all.

Willy had gotten up early and dressed quietly. Then he'd made two peanut butter sandwiches, filled his battered thermos with last night's warm tea, put the lunch in his backpack, closed the door softly and set off for the far end of the island.

Grandmother was ill and Willy knew this would be their last winter together. For a long time, he had tried to think of a gift he could bring to her. It would have to be special. Finally he decided and made his careful plan.

The heavy, gray sky stretched over the land. Looking back he could no longer see the village. For one awful moment, he felt like running back to the safety and warmth of Grandmother's old house. Instead, he took a deep breath, looked at his pocket compass, and set off toward the distant coast with a more determined step.

A sudden wind hit Willy like a spray of ice water. He shivered and pulled his furry parka hood close around his face. Peering into the gathering fog, he felt himself being swallowed by a hungry white monster. His heart began to beat painfully in his chest. Then he remembered the talk he'd had with Grandmother last night.

He could almost see her, almost hear her speaking. "Willy," she'd said, "when I'm afraid, I remind myself that I can always trust my spirit helpers to be here with me."

Suddenly, Willy felt safe. "Yes," he told himself, "it's foolish to be frightened. I'm not alone. My spirit helpers are here with me."

At last he reached the coast. He looked out at the green-gray sea. The water came rolling up over the rocky shore. Then he sat down to eat his lunch.

Willy sat for a long time, watching the sea as it reached up to grasp the land only to fall back again and gather itself up for another rush up the battered rocks.

Then he began walking up the shore looking for the cobblestone cove. After a few minutes, he reached that particular place where the water had tumbled the rocks in a manner that made the beach appear paved with round stones. Then he began to search for the most beautiful one.

Finally Willy selected a smooth, round, black stone and wrapped it in his scarf. He placed it in his backpack and turned back toward home.

A couple of hours later, Grandmother saw him returning. She saw how he held his shoulders square as he picked his way confidently across the familiar frozen landscape. She could tell it had been a good day for Willy.

While Willy warmed himself near the wood-burning cook stove, Grandmother pressed fresh bread dough into small biscuits. Later, they dipped the warm bread into steaming bowls of bean soup and sipped cups of honey-sweetened tea. Grandmother was beginning her second cup when Willy pushed himself away from the table.

Quietly he lifted his backpack from its peg on the wall and carried it to the table. Reaching into the backpack he pulled out his bulging scarf and placed it in front of Grandmother.

Slowly she opened the bundle and picked up the stone. She closed her fingers around it and held it tight.

Willy watched with pride and quiet excitement. The stone looked so smooth and shiny in Grandmother's small thin hand.

As she listened to it tell the secrets that only a stone can tell, Grandmother smiled at having received such a wonderful gift.

Then she smiled at Willy. Her tired eyes were bright with happiness because she knew what the stone had cost him and what it had taught him.

"Yes," Willy thought, "this is a perfect gift."

Where Does
the Train Go?

WHEN I WAS still too young to go to school we lived near the railroad tracks in Fosston, Minnesota. I learned to love the red caboose and the dark hissing steam engines. When the train arrived I watched carefully. I saw the busy workers add coal and water to make the steam that made the power that ran the great engine. Soon the train was on its way again.

"Good bye! Good bye!" it seemed to say as it chugged out of sight.

"Good bye!" I shouted to the red caboose.

Then one day I asked Mama, "Where does the train go?"

But Mama was making bread and didn't want to talk about trains.

I asked Dad, "Where does the train go?"

But Dad was building a rabbit hutch and didn't have time to talk about trains.

I asked Grandpa Louie, "Where does the train go?"

"Far away," he said in a wistful voice.

The next day Mama heard the same question again. She heard it the next day, and the next.

At last she told me, "Tomorrow I'll sell some eggs and we'll go for a ride on the train. Then you'll know where the train goes."

I told my rabbit about the plan. "Isn't it wonderful?"

The rabbit stared at me without blinking and wiggled his pink nose. Then he kicked at his ear with his hind foot and said, "Wonderful."

"I can't wait until tomorrow," I confided in our dog, Sneeze. "I'm going where the train goes."

Sneeze was so excited by this news that he stood on his back legs and danced in circles, while singing a happy song.

Finally the long day was over and I laid my tired head on the plump pillow. Before I could wonder about the grand event of the coming day, I was asleep.

The next day Mama and I boarded the train and took our seats. I sat near the window so I could see everything. Mama read the names of the towns along the way. "Bagley... Shevlin... Solway... Wilton..."

We got off the train at Bemidji and went into the depot. Dad was sitting on a long bench waiting for us.

Before returning to Fosston in our old truck, Dad stopped at a drug store and bought three ice cream cones.

As I licked away the ice cream I thought, "Now I know where the train goes." This was all I would ever want to know. It seemed that such joy would last forever. Then I nibbled away the cone.

Several weeks passed as I continued to welcome the trains into Fosston and wave them out of town.

Then one day I asked, "Mama, where does the train come from?"

Indian School Runaway

SEVEN-YEAR-OLD Charlie Blue ran down a narrow road clad only in a pair of faded pants and a thin cotton shirt. He carefully avoided soft or dusty places, where his feet would leave tracks.

He glanced over his shoulder when he heard a wagon coming then dove headlong into a ditch, scrambled through the low brush and hid behind a fallen tree.

He'd been running for a long time, so he lay there for several minutes pressing his fingers against the persistent ache deep in his abdomen.

Looking up he saw a few ripe raspberries hanging overhead. Without rising he picked all within his reach and ate them carefully, savoring each bite. "Thank you, Creator, for feeding this pitiful one," he prayed.

For several minutes, he watched the intense sun shining through the tops of the trees, and listened to the song of the leaves. His eyes followed a hungry woodpecker as it flew from tree to tree in search of food. Then he rose to his knees and crept toward the road.

Later, as he lay in the tall grass, he thought of his family. He imagined how glad they would be to see him. A smile spread over his dirty face. Then he turned over and laid his head on his thin arms and closed his eyes. He tried to stay awake, but a diet of beans and government gravy will keep a boy weak and tired. Soon he was asleep.

Suddenly he was jerked to his feet and struck several times about his head. He raised his arms to protect his face and was flung to the ground. A heavy boot pressed down on his back.

"Watcha doin', boy?" a menacing male voice asked. "Runnin' from the injun school? Don't you know ole Dan Mann is too smart for ya? Don't ya know I'm waitin' for ya? I can catch ya ever' time. 'Specially ya little ones. Ya'll so dumb."

Rolling the boy over with his foot the man looked at him more closely. Dropping to one knee he grabbed Charlie by the hair, pulling him forward until their noses nearly touched. The boy could smell the unwashed white man's sour breath and body odors.

"Well now, ain't ya the purdy un? That ole priest'll give twen'y bucks to have ya back," he growled.

Then he yanked Charlie to his feet. The boy didn't know which way to run and before he could decide, the man had tied him hand and foot, and dragged him down the road.

A team of horses and a wagon were hidden in the tall bushes. The man tossed Charlie into the wagon box. Then he heaved himself up into the seat and slapped the reins down on the horses' quivering rumps.

When the wagon lurched forward Charlie tumbled backwards and struck his head on something sharp. He felt the warm blood trickle through his hair as hungry flies began arriving for a midday feast.

Old Dan Mann took Charlie back to the school, presented him to the grateful priest and collected the 20-dollar reward.

But the next time Charlie tried to rejoin his family and the comfort of their warm affection, the priest beat him with a stout stick and sent him back to the dormitory.

Later, in the quiet darkness of the little boys' sleeping quarters, Father Marcel arrived for a midnight visit. The priest was small, with a pale complexion, long thin fingers and blond curling hair.

He kissed the small boy, begging him to be good. "Don't run away from me, little one. I love you. Do you love me?"

Charlie tried to say "yes," but he could not.

"Tell me," the priest pleaded. "Tell me that you love me."

"No," said the boy. "I don't."

The priest winced, rose from the bed and stepped quietly out of the room.

"It's over," Charlie thought. Relieved and exhausted, he fell into a fitful sleep.

Before breakfast Father Marcel sent for the runaway. Two older boys escorted Charlie to a small room in the dank basement. A heavy wooden chair stood in the middle of the brick floor.

Johnny Smith looked Charlie over with a smirk and tried to kiss him. Charlie resisted and spat in the big boy's face.

The other boy stepped forward as a fist shot toward Charlie. Then the other boy grabbed Johnny and twisted his arm so hard that the big boy moaned and fell to his knees.

"Leave him alone," Joe Thunder said.

"What do you care how I treat him," Johnny demanded.

"Because he's my friend," Joe said.

Charlie was surprised. He didn't know he had a friend. But before he could savor the moment, the door burst open and Father Marcel entered.

He told the big boys to return to their morning chores and closed the heavy door behind them.

After locking the door, the priest turned to Charlie. "Strip," he ordered in a cold, calm voice.

With trembling fingers Charlie removed his clothes, dropping them in a heap on the damp bricks. Father Marcel placed Charlie in the chair backwards. Then he tied his hands and feet, binding the boy so tightly to the chair that he could not move.

Afterwards, the priest clasped his hands behind his back and paced around the room for several minutes.

At last, he spoke in a soft, pleasant voice. "I know why you run away. It's because the devils tell you to do this bad thing. All of you poor Indian children are full of devils when you're born. It's up to me to get those devils out of you before they ruin your lives."

Then the priest took a wide leather strap from a hook near the door. "I'll have to beat them out of you. Then you'll be my good little boy and you'll stop trying to run away."

The boy clenched his teeth. "I won't cry," he told himself.

But when the strap fell, a pitiful scream ripped through Charlie's throat.

Father Marcel was delighted. "There goes one of those dirty devils!"

So Charlie screamed with every blow until he fainted.

He awakened in the infirmary. He tried to get up, but the effort was met with excruciating pain. He lay on his face gasping into the white sheet. When he was able to focus his eyes, he saw that he was isolated behind white fabric screens.

He lay there for hours. Not moving. Not weeping. Not thinking. The smell of alcohol and disinfectants pinched his nose.

At last one of the screens opened and a nun stepped toward him. With gentle hands she raised his head and placed a towel under his face. Patiently she spooned chicken broth into his hungry mouth.

Then she left without speaking. Carefully she closed the screen behind her. Her quiet steps grew faint and disappeared into a heavy silence. Charlie wondered if she knew about the midnight visits.

Did she know he was full of devils?

Abducted

H E'D APPEARED suddenly among us in his dusty clothes and loose soiled shirt. His hair was long and greasy under his dirty red baseball cap. Like a long lost relative, he'd come to our door on a Sunday afternoon.

"Good afternoon, Ma'am," he said when Mama opened the door about a foot and looked out at him. He let a friendly grin slide across his narrow face. "Drove all the way from Tennessee looking for an old friend."

Granny and I didn't go to the door. We looked at the tall lean stranger from the window.

We looked at each other and scowled. We wondered how he'd made such a long trip in that beat up car. It didn't sound like it would go much farther.

Then Papa went to the door and pulled it wide open. The man removed his cap and said he was looking for a fellow he'd met during the war. He told Papa they'd marched all over Europe together.

"He's a liar," Granny whispered loudly. "Look at his feet. Flat footed and pigeon toed. Why, he couldn't march to the outhouse."

Then she poked me in the ribs with her painfully sharp elbow. "Never trust a liar, Lizzy," she hissed through clenched teeth. Then holding her face close to mine she peered into my eyes. Then she pulled herself up as tall as possible and shaking her finger in my face she said, "Never. Never. Never."

The liar was still talking. So we pulled the curtain back to get a better look at him.

"Would you happen to know Gordon Phillips?" he asked tentatively as he waved the red cap before his sweaty face.

Mama and Papa looked at each other then shook their heads in unison. Nobody knew Gordon Phillips.

"'Course not," Granny huffed. "That's part of his big lie."

"He said if I ever got to Bagley, Minnesota, that I should look him up. Well, here I am." He grinned again to show his good teeth. "Looks like I came a long way for nothin.'"

"Never been any Phillips around here," Granny muttered. "Never."

"Well," he drawled, looking south. "It's a long way back to Tennessee."

He scratched his head and looked at Mama, "Well, I guess I better be gettin' on my way."

No one objected, so he was already in the car before Mama raised her voice and said something we'll never forget. "Wanna stay for supper?"

Mama was like that. She wanted to feed all the bums. She brought in stray cats and lost dogs and weary strangers. She never could send a hungry dog or a skinny cat down the road without trying to feed it first.

"Shoot!" Granny grumped. "He won't leave now." I watched her skinny figure climb the stairs to her room. She seemed lost in the colorful folds of her calico dress.

The man hesitated briefly, then got out of his car and came into our home. I went up to my room until Mama called me down for supper. Granny wanted to eat in her room and I did, too. Mama frowned, but carried a tray up for Granny and I took up a tray for myself. I sat quiet, waiting for Granny to say something more about the stranger. But she was quiet, too.

After supper Papa cleaned out a small shed and fixed up a cot for the stranger. He even apologized because the shed was small and had no door. Mama brought out an old army blanket and Papa nailed it up where the door should have been.

The man's name was Clayton E. Bradshaw. He seemed mighty proud of it, too. It rolled off his tongue about 30 times a day.

The man mowed the grass, split wood to fill the pole barn for winter and hauled water, too. So Mama let him stay on a few days more than we thought he should.

Granny didn't like the man. In fact, she seemed to hate him. I decided that I didn't like him either. I was twelve years old that summer and Granny was my best friend. She'd come to live with us when Grandpa Tripp died. Mama was her only child.

"He can't fool me. That man is no good. There's something evil about his eyes. They're always moving. Like he's looking for something—or looking for someone—and it's not Gordon Phillips. You stay away from him, Lizzy," she said.

I didn't like his gray washed-out eyes either. I stayed away from him.

Well, it turned out that Granny was right about Bradshaw. He was looking for someone—and he found her. My cousin Harriet had just turned thirteen that year. We had already made summer plans and they didn't include being kidnapped.

But that's just what happened! Clayton E. Bradshaw plucked Harriet right out from under our noses and carried her off.

Of course, it was reported and the cops started looking for her. They even came looking in our woodshed, which I thought was pretty dumb.

"Those cops couldn't find their buns if they weren't sitting on them most of the time," Uncle Elmer fumed.

"I want my girl!" Auntie Em cried.

Granny stayed in her room and prayed.

After a week or so the cops agreed that Harriet and Bradshaw were not in the area and the manhunt broadened.

The law had opened a tired eye and seen an injustice. The perpetrator would be charged with kidnapping a minor and taking her across state lines. Bradshaw was going to do time. But first he had to be apprehended.

About six weeks later Uncle Elmer got a phone call from Missouri. Harriet had been found and hospitalized. She was being treated for trauma, dehydration and malnutrition. Uncle Elmer and Auntie Em were relieved but frightened. They drove down to get her at once. Bradshaw would go to prison and none of us would ever see him again. I think he died there.

When Harriet came home she was changed. She'd left us as a young and carefree girl and returned an old woman. She didn't want to go swimming or riding bikes. Nor did she want to build the tree house, which had been her own idea! She just wanted to sit alone in her room. When school started we could see that things were going to be different. Most of the girls didn't speak to Harriet anymore and the boys said nasty things about her.

"Lizzy," Granny said, "you be nice to Harriet. What happened to her wasn't her fault."

To tell the truth, I really didn't know what had happened to Harriet. But I knew it had to be something pretty bad.

I was never unkind to her. But I still wanted to ride a bike, swim, build a tree house and steal apples. When we weren't in school, Harriet stayed in the house most of the time. It was hard on our friendship.

Then Uncle Elmer and Auntie Em decided to sell out and leave. They wanted to start a new life in a new place. Uncle Elmer gave Papa his carpenter tools.

"I got a job welding," he said. "I have no use for these and I know you have a lot of improvements you want to make on this old place," he said as he slapped Papa on the back.

Mama wept when Auntie Em gave her a box of wedding china. "It's so fragile," Em said. "It would just get broken along the way."

They hired a neighbor with a truck to move them to Minneapolis. They didn't even come back for a visit. Mama and Auntie Em exchanged letters but Harriet didn't write to me. Sometimes Granny got a birthday card or a valentine from her.

It was Granny who kept Harriet alive for me. She'd remember funny things that happened when we were little kids together. Sometimes I'd laugh until I cried because she made the stories so funny. Talking about Harriet made it seem like she might come home someday.

Well, they stayed away for about nine years and returned for Granny's funeral. Granny just got sick and died. It was all quite sudden. Mama said she was glad Granny hadn't suffered for a long time. We all missed her. I knew I'd lost my best forever-friend.

Harriet returned for the funeral.

I was twenty-one then and working in the elementary school kitchen. Harriet was married and had two pretty little girls. Arlene was eight and Bertha was two. Her husband, Toby, was a small quiet man.

After the funeral, graveside service and reception, Harriet came over and took my hand. "I always liked her, Lizzy. She was nice to me even when I came back from Missouri."

I couldn't speak without crying so I sat in silence. Harriet embraced me and asked if she could come over to see me the following day.

"I'll leave the girls with Toby and drive over. We can go for a ride and find a place to talk. I want to tell you about the abduction."

I was surprised. "Oh, Harriet, you don't have to tell me anything."

"I know," she said. "But I want to."

She came about 11 a.m. A picnic hamper sat in the back seat of her car. Next to the hamper sat Granny. I guess I should have been surprised but I wasn't.

Harriet drove fast, but I liked it. Granny was grinning and clinging to the door handle.

We went to a quiet wooded area close to a small lake, spread the blanket on the ground and emptied the hamper.

Granny sat on one corner of the blanket. After we'd eaten, Harriet squared her shoulders, took a deep breath and began telling me the story of her ordeal.

It had begun almost immediately. Bradshaw kept telling her how pretty she was and was always trying to hold her hand. She couldn't come over to see me because she didn't want him to bother her.

Then one day he found her walking along the road near her house. He offered her a ride but she kept walking. He stopped the car and jumped out. She ran but he caught her and dragged her back to the car. He hit her in the face with his fist.

When she awakened she was inside the dark dusty trunk of the dirty old car. She began kicking and screaming. The car stopped and Bradshaw opened the trunk and yelled at her. "Shut up, you ugly little bitch! I'll kill you if I have to!"

Granny winced and covered her face.

"I don't care!" Harriet had shouted back at him. He hit her again.

When she woke up he was dragging her out of the trunk. He flung her to the ground and raped her. That was the first time—but not the last.

What she said next gave me a better understanding of why Granny hated Bradshaw from the first time she saw him.

"I guess you know she was abducted, too," Harriet said. "She was only twelve years old. Just a little girl, Lizzy. A tiny little girl."

"No," I admitted. "I didn't know."

That night I dreamed about Granny. Saw her being carried away by Clayton E. Bradshaw. Heard her crying and begging for help. "Lizzy! Lizzy!" she screamed.

But it was Harriet who swooped out of the darkness and snatched Granny away from Bradshaw. The two girls held hands as they ran. When he chased after them, they turned and jumped on him. They beat him into the ground with their small bloody fists.

Mama awakened me, shaking my shoulders. She pulled me into her arms and held me tight.

"Mama, why didn't you tell me about Granny?"

"She never wanted you to know."

"Why not?"

"To protect us." Mama lowered her head and spoke almost to herself. "Didn't want you to know that your mama was the offspring of a man who stole her from her home in North Carolina and left her pregnant beside the road in Kansas."

"How'd she get to Minnesota?"

"Your Grandpa Tripp found her. She wouldn't go back to North Carolina, so he brought her home and his mother took care of her. After I was born, they got married. She never had any other children. Just me."

"Oh, Mama," I wept.

"But it's all right now. Don't you see?"

I shook my head.

"Your Grandpa Tripp loved her. She loved him. Then they loved me. Then we all loved you. So, you see, it's really a love story, after all."

Dad's Best Shirt

IT WAS SHORTLY after the funeral and I was packing Dad's clothes.

"Sissy," he'd told me, "I want all my clothes to go to the boys at the halfway house. Sometimes those poor guys come in with just the clothes on their backs. It's especially difficult to find clothes for big men—like me."

Over the years he'd added a bit of variety to his basic brown wardrobe. Among his beige and tan shirts were some green and gold ones, too. But when I found the lavender shirt in the bottom drawer of his beat up bureau, I buried my face in its familiar folds and sat down on the creaky old bed. Weeping quietly I remembered how that old shirt had come to be among his most precious possessions.

I was twelve years old and it was almost Father's Day. So I was shopping for Dad at the second-hand store. My younger brother Bones was shopping, too. He was probably about five then.

His real name was Carson but he fell off the porch when he was a baby and fractured his arm. So we called him Little Broken Bones. Afterwards we shortened it to Bones. Daddy always teased Bones. Said he was homely 'cause his ears stuck out. Mama disagreed.

"Your ears stick out, too," she reminded Dad. "But we don't call you homely."

We women-folk always thought Bones was real cute.

"Bones," I asked, "what are you getting for Dad?"

"Something that costs a whole dime," was all he would say.

"I got a quarter. We could pool our money and get something for 35 cents," I suggested.

Bones puckered up his little face to consider the offer. Then he said, "No, thank you. I wanna get something that's just from me."

I smiled to myself and thought, "We have got us a real bright boy."

I'd told him many times, "Carson, when I get to be a mother I want a little boy just like you."

He'd grin and wrinkle his nose and I'd just about die for joy. Then I'd hug him tight and kiss him up. Oh, he'd laugh and laugh! Yep, that's just how it was. I couldn't help myself. I loved that boy!

Suddenly I saw just what Dad needed! I took it to the store-keep and plunked down my money. "How much?" I asked.

"Well," she considered, "I usually get fifty cents for those big shirts. But I know your dad needs a good-looking shirt and it is Father's Day. So I'll take the quarter and call us square."

Just then Bones came to the counter carrying a coffee mug decorated with an Irish Setter. He stood on his toes, put the mug on the counter and opened his small hand to show his dime. I knew those mugs cost twenty-five cents, but the store-keep said, "That's just enough!"

She wrapped the mug in newspaper, put it in a sack and gave it to Bones. When he smiled up at her, she smiled back, opened the sack and put two pieces of penny candy inside.

Walking home was fun that day. Miz Loretta T. Jones was out in her yard when we passed her house.

"Say," she asked me, "where did you get such a nice little brother?"

"Second-hand store," I told her. "They're two for a nickel this week. But I got the last one for half price."

Miz Jones' soft laughter came from way down in her belly. We listened to it rumble, rise slowly into her throat and exit from her large mouth. She made us laugh, too.

Then she patted Bones on the head and told me, "You keep an eye on this half-price boy, you hear. We don't want anyone stealing him."

When we got home, Mama wanted to see what we'd purchased. We opened our packages and stood back to wait for her approval.

"Bones," she said with pride and pleasure, "you're a real good shopper. This cup is the perfect Father's Day gift!"

To me she said, "Why on earth did you get your father a purple shirt? He won't wear it."

"This is not a purple shirt," I informed her. "It's lavender."

"Well, he won't wear it," she repeated. "He's got a drawer full of brown shirts 'cause that's the only color he likes. You should have got him a brown shirt."

"He's already got too many brown shirts, Mama! It's time he tried something different. Something bright and colorful."

"Well," she muttered. "It is that."

Just then Bones spoke up. "I like it," he said.

So Mama and I stopped fighting, and laughed together over our bright little Bones. Then Bones and I decorated a couple of brown paper sacks with crayon designs, wrapped our gifts and tied them tight with store strings. We'd found a dead robin that morning, so I stuck a few feathers in the knots.

"Sissy," Mama said, "those feathers add a nice touch. You're a real artist."

The next morning we fixed breakfast for Dad and he ate in bed. Then we gave him his gifts. He opened Bones' package first. Oh! Dad loved that mug!

"I used to have a dog who looked just like that," he told us.

"Mama!" he shouted toward the kitchen. "Do you remember my dog, Red?"

But Mama didn't answer 'cause she was pretending not to listen. So Dad went on talking about his old dog.

"Red was real talented. He used to cook for me." Just then Mama stepped into the room so Dad added, "Of course, that was before I married your mother. She cooks better than any dog I ever knew."

Bones and I laughed at the idea of a dog cooking for Dad.

"Yeah," Mama muttered, "I saw some of those dogs."

Then Bones and I laughed even harder. But Mama didn't even smile. So Dad tried to make her laugh, too.

"Red could drive a car, too," he told us in his most sincere voice. "Mama still doesn't know how to drive," he whispered out loud.

"Sometimes when I'd had a little too much to drink he'd drive me home," Dad said with a wink. "He'd bring me right to the door. Then he'd take off with my car and pick up all his fleabag buddies. They'd drive around all night long! But I never had to worry, 'cause Red didn't drink."

Bones fell on his side laughing at the images Dad's stories had conjured up in his little boy head. Oh, it was so funny! But Mama didn't laugh at all.

So Dad went on telling us about that dog. "Red's best trick was talking like Ed Sullivan. I had him call your mother once, and when I got home she was acting proud and sassy. She told me she'd been on the phone with a famous TV personality." That did it! Mama's face cracked into a big smile and she slapped Dad with her dishtowel. "You're a damned liar!" she said.

Then he opened my package, held up the shirt and whistled. "Sissy," he said, "I have never seen such a beautiful shirt. I'll save it for special."

That's what he did, too. That lavender shirt showed up for all my birthdays, at Christmas and on Father's Day. He wore it just three times a year.

"That way I won't wear it out," he'd told me many times. "I want to keep this one for the rest of my life."

Now there I sat blowing my nose on Dad's best shirt.

Just then Bones came in to see what was taking so long. When he saw the lavender shirt he folded his six-foot plus frame, sat down and put his arm around me.

"I'm not sure I can send this one to the half-way house," I told him tearfully.

"Well. Sissy," he said, "you don't have to. I want you to know that I have always admired this lavender shirt. So, if you don't mind, I'll just take it home with me and wear it for special."

Then I fell into his arms and we sat on the edge of Dad's old bed, laughing through our tears.

Junkyard Deal

AMANDA WAS fascinated by the junkyard with its ten-foot high fortress of rotting boards. They'd been painted blood red once, but most of the blood was gone now. She loved the tall silver-weathered boards held together with bits of rusting iron. Sometimes it looked like a sad old ship and she imagined how it was lost on a stormy sea. She seemed to remember how the tide had retreated, leaving the ship stuck on Cedar Avenue.

Amanda loved the old junkyard and she loved junk. Although she had an impressive collection for an eight-year-old, the box under her bed seemed very small compared to the wealth that Junkman possessed. So she couldn't help but envy him for having such a vast amount of that wonderful stuff.

Of course, the treasures had to be protected. So Junkman had "no trespassing" signs posted all around and three large dogs to frighten nighttime intruders away. But he kept the fierce beasts on a short chain during the day.

So it was her love of junk that drove her to do something almost unthinkable. She decided to visit the junkyard alone. This was something none of the kids she knew had ever done before. It took a lot of courage, but she did it.

She approached the junkyard in a nonchalant manner, looking up at the sky and whistling softly until Junkman went off with a customer. Then she ducked quickly through the tall gate that kept trespassers out. She, of course, was not a trespasser. She was an admirer. That sign was for boys like Ike, Gary and Dick, who often came to break glass and steal hubcaps.

Stealthily she crept behind a pile of rotting auto innards and scurried about like a sewer rat until she found a car she really liked. Then she sat down behind the steering wheel and began the long drive to Kalamazoo.

"My, my," she told herself, "It's a fine day for a trip. But I hope it doesn't take too long because I can't be late for lunch. I'm dining at The Grand Hotel with Clark Gable today and he hates it when I'm late."

She was driving pretty fast so she slowed down to cross the Golden Gate Bridge and get a better view of Lady Liberty standing out on Coney Island. Although she was familiar with several important landmarks, she wasn't particularly interested in their actual location and frequently made serious errors in her geography. None of which troubled her in the least.

"Why must she look so sad? If we must have statues standing in the ocean why can't they be beautiful and happy like Carmen Miranda or Doris Day?"

Growing tired of her fantasy she pulled the big car to a quick stop and said, "Well, here we are in Kalamazoo!"

Suddenly a big surly face was staring at her through the windshield, and it didn't look like Clark Gable. Before she could escape Junkman had her by the arm.

"Let me go!" she shouted. "I'm late for lunch."

"Well, so am I, Miss Kalamazoo," Junkman growled.

He took her to his office and plunked her down on his car seat sofa. Amanda caressed the coffee-tan texture of the upholstery with one hand while the other explored the shiny coolness of the chrome ashtray built into the leather armrest. Junkman watched her closely.

"I'm turning you over to the law," he said as he reached for the phone.

Amanda was surprised. "Why? I haven't done any harm. I didn't break anything and I didn't steal anything."

Junkman seemed to forget the phone for the moment as he focused on the girl. "You're the one that's been breaking windows and stealing hubcaps!" he accused angrily.

Amanda had been shouted at most of her life so she was not intimidated by loud angry voices. "No! I am not!" she said. "But I know who they are."

Junkman leaned forward as Amanda spilled her guts. "It was Ike, Gary and Dick," she ratted.

"Are they your friends?" Junkman asked.

"No," she lied. "I hardly know them."

Amanda didn't like to lie but self-preservation is a powerful instinct.

Junkman stared at her for a long uncomfortable minute. Then he said, "Wanna make a deal?"

Amanda wasn't sure she wanted to make a deal with Junkman but he had her in a compromising position. "Okay," she said reluctantly, "Whaddya want?"

Junkman licked his lips and spoke softly. "I'll give you anything you can carry out of the yard. Anything."

She was definitely interested now. Like a panther her mind went slipping in and out of cars until she found the one that held the greatest treasure. She'd seen it one day when she was exploring with the boys.

Junkman went on. "You tell those boys that you came here today and I turned the dogs loose. Tell them that you ran up on the top of the old bus where they couldn't reach you. Tell them that they growled and snarled and leaped at you."

Amanda glanced down at the three tired dogs on the floor at her feet.

"Then tell them that I dragged you down from the bus and kicked your ass all the way to the gate. Will you do it?"

"Sure," she agreed. "It's a real good idea."

Junkman smiled shyly at her sincere compliment and said, "Okay, Kalamazoo. Whaddya want?"

Amanda led him straight to the car that held the prize and pointed to the green glass stick shift knob.

"You pack a mean deal," Junkman told her. Carefully he removed the elegant knob and held it in front of Amanda. "Ain't it a beauty?" he marveled. "See how the fine lines of cream swirl up out of the jade? It's like a sweet mist rising from a green sea."

"Yeah," Amada sighed. "A real gem."

Then they walked back to the office where Junkman polished the knob and placed it in Amanda's waiting hand. Then he walked her to the gate. "All right, Kalamazoo, get out of here. And don't you ever let me catch you in my yard again."

"It's a deal," she promised.

She was almost home when she saw Ike and Gary and Dick coming toward her. Quickly she put the knob in her pocket and began limping painfully along.

"Hey Amanda!" Ike called. "Where ya been?"

"I went to the junkyard," she moaned, her face twisted in agony, "those mean old dogs scared the hell out of me. I had to climb up on that old bus to stay alive! They were barking and growling and trying to reach me with their long bloody fangs. Then Junkman dragged me down and kicked my ass all the way to the gate."

"Holy crap!" Ike said with sudden respect. "Are you all right?"

Amanda grimaced, "Oh, yeah. I guess I'll be all right in a few days."

As she limped along she added, "You know that Junkman wears steel-toed boots and kicks like a mule."

Then she slipped her hand into her pocket and wrapped her fingers around the green glass sea.

Shattered Trust

M Y MOTHER had already divorced my father and remarried so I didn't see too much of him. But when I was about twelve years old, Dad had a small truck market where he sold produce in Minneapolis.

I often spent part of the summer in St Paul with my Aunt Gerry and her family. He would come to visit me there and he often brought a little gift. My mother usually didn't allow me to go anywhere with him at that time because she said he was "unreliable."

But one day, Dad came to my Aunt Gerry's home in St. Paul and asked if I could go to work with him. The produce stand was located somewhere around Lake Calhoun in Minneapolis.

Aunt Gerry didn't want me to go, but I begged her until she gave up in disgust and said, "All right! But if anything should happen, call me. I'll come and get you."

"What could possibly go wrong?" I wondered as I hurried away with Dad.

It was always fun to go with him. He liked to try everything. Nothing seemed to frighten him. He didn't worry about practical things. Some people thought he was a bit reckless. He said, "I'm living for the moment!"

It was sunny and nicely warm, so a lot of people stopped to look at our produce. Some of them bought a little and some of them bought a lot.

It was mid-afternoon when Dad said, "I'll have to get some change. You keep the store open. When I get back we'll work a couple of more hours, and then I'll take you out for supper," he promised.

I kept watching and waiting but he didn't return. At last I took some coins and went out to find a pay phone.

I called Aunt Gerry. "Dad left me out here," I told her.

She was furious. "I'm coming right now. Lock yourself inside and don't open the door until I get there."

I returned to "the store," as Dad called the little roadside stand, and started putting the produce inside. The night had grown chilly, the mosquitoes were hungry and I was alone with my shattered trust and broken heart.

When Aunt Gerry arrived, she scolded me for being concerned about the produce. "Let it rot," she seethed.

"He's got to make a living," I said.

Then I put the money in the metal box and hid it under the counter where Dad could find it when he came back to work.

Again she scolded me. "Take that money! You're the one who earned it. He already took his share."

So I took a few dollars to satisfy her.

It was a quiet ride back to the house. I tried to pretend that being abandoned by my father didn't bother me, but Aunt Gerry knew how deeply I'd been hurt.

"You know what happened, don't you?" she asked.

"Yes," I answered.

He'd taken the money to buy a bottle, and his prosperity got the best of him. With money in his pocket, he'd found friends.

I could hear him, making his old excuses. "I just couldn't leave while I still had money. The boys would do the same for me. Well, you're a big girl! I figured you could take care of yourself, and you did just fine."

The truth was hard to take. He'd simply forgotten all about me, waiting alone in the cold night.

But I knew he'd wake up sick and sorry. He'd be ashamed, too.

"I won't hear from him again," I told my aunt, "not for a long, long time."

"That's right," she replied, "And don't you feel sorry for him either."

But I did and I do and I always will.

Good Choice!

FUNNY-HONEY BOY was hungry. He'd been playing for hours and his breakfast was all gone. He could feel the empty place in his belly where the eggs and toast had been. He knew his mother would be getting lunch ready soon and although she was moving at a brisk pace it wasn't swift enough for him. To get his mind off his stomach he decided to go for a quick walk and return when lunch was on the table.

As he went along Shannon Lane he met a stranger dressed in black leotards and silver slippers. The man was very tall and quite thin. In fact, he was skinny. He wore a long tomato red cape that floated about him in a saucy manner. The front of the cape was festooned with a garland of garlic and onions of all sizes. His head was encircled with a wreath of delicately fragrant mushrooms and he carried a long wooden spoon that he used for a walking stick. The handle was engraved with mythical kitchen symbols.

"What a fine looking chap," the boy thought. "And how brave to be walking around in that outrageous get-up."

But the boy was attracted to the man and wanted to know who he was. "Excuse me, Sir," he said, "but I don't think I've ever seen you here before."

"I'm not surprised," the man replied. "I've never been here before and since you don't look like a wandering lad, I'm quite sure this is the first time we've ever met."

Then without removing his wreath and bending very low, he bowed before the boy until his nose was touching the ground. Returning to an upright position he folded his long arms across his narrow chest and said, "I can tell by your fine bright eyes that you can see I am a man of great dignity and extreme kindness. Perhaps you see that I am also a magician."

Actually, the boy could see no such thing but not wanting to disappoint the stranger, he said, "Quite right, old man."

"I am also an excellent cook," the man boasted. "But now I'd like to know more about you. What is your favorite food?"

Without hesitation the boy said, "Macaroni!"

"Good choice!" the tall man shouted and clapped his hands together so fast that blue sparks shot from his fingertips. "It just happens that I am the King of Macaroni."

Now the boy was quite surprised by this announcement because he didn't know there was such a thing as the King of Macaroni. But he didn't want the man to know he didn't know so he smiled serenely and the man went on speaking.

"With your macaroni... do you like tomatoes or cheese?" the man asked.

"Well," the boy thought and pulled his ear for a minute. Then he said, "I actually like both. But this week I have a slight preference for tomatoes."

"Good choice!" the man sang out. "However, there are other things you can put on your macaroni and tomatoes. Some children like hamburger. Some like bacon. What do you like?"

"Well," the boy said, "I prefer neither."

"Good choice!" the man shouted again. "But a little flavor should not be neglected my fine lad. Would you prefer onions or garlic?"

"Today I prefer both," the boy told him.

"Good choice!" the man said as he jumped up and down several times. He jumped very high and each time he came down the silver slippers emitted a musical cloud of tiny tinkles.

Then he whisked the boy off his feet and carried him across the sky to the Macaroni Mountains where the great Macaroni Castle stood in a field of ruffled green parsley.

They hurried to the tall spaghetti gate, crossed the cheesy moat and entered the unprotected pasta premises. Down the halls they scurried until they reached the elegant dining room where several robust and mustached macaroni chefs were waiting. They tugged their bow ties as they winked and grinned.

"My young friend would like a macaroni lunch prepared with tomatoes, garlic and onions," the King said.

The chefs smiled at the boy. "Good choice!" they said in unison and hurried away to the kitchen, where they disappeared into a burst of rosy steam.

At that moment the boy remembered that his mother was preparing lunch for him so he turned to his host and said, "Please, forgive me but I must go home at once."

"Right away!" the King replied. "But first I have a gift for you. You see, I have been searching for the Macaroni Kid and I have no doubt my quest ends here! Therefore, I give you this small crown of royal macaroni and the penne decree that pronounces you the one and only true Macaroni Kid."

"Good choice!" said the boy with no sense of unworthiness.

The King pressed the crown onto the boy's head and put the decree in his hand. Then he touched the boy on the nose with his magic bread stick and immediately the boy was back in his own house at his own table where his mother was putting down a plate of steaming macaroni.

He peered closely at the fragrant food to evaluate its quality. It was smothered deliciously in tomatoes, garlic and onions. Just the way he liked it. He gave his mother a nod of approval and said, "Thanks Mom! I'm starved."

His mother leaned down, removed his macaroni crown and kissed him on the nose.

"Mom," he said. "You're my favorite cook!"

"Good choice!" she said. Then she sang and danced around the kitchen juggling three bread sticks while the Macaroni Kid licked the platter clean.

Then he put on his crown and his mother fixed his royal title to the refrigerator door with a macaroni magnet. Afterwards she put on her silver slippers and they went out to pick a basket of ruffled green parsley.

Charlie's Beans

THE NEIGHBORHOOD children had chosen sides for a softball game but no one wanted Charlie on their team. Even his two older brothers didn't want him to play.

"You're just too small to play," said Steven.

"You can't run," said Tom.

Charlie wandered into our small garden, "Mom, can I help you?" he asked.

I looked toward the sunny field where the softball players were taking their positions. "Oh, Charlie," I said, "I really need help with the beans. Can you be in charge of them?"

"Sure, Mom," he beamed.

Charlie listened carefully to my instructions. Soon he'd dug a shallow L-shaped trench along two sides of the garden.

I cut a stick four inches long and showed Charlie how to space the beans. Then I cut a notch in one end of the stick to show how deep to plant the beans. "They should be about four inches apart and one inch deep," I explained.

Charlie did just as he was told. If the trench was too deep, he added dirt. If the trench was too shallow, he scooped dirt out. Then he laid the beans in the trench and I inspected his work.

"Well done!" I shouted proudly.

Then, on my knees, I showed Charlie how to cover the beans. Carefully he refilled the trench and pressed the cool, damp soil down firmly with his hand.

When he finished, I gave him a small package of marigold seeds. "They look like fat eyelashes," he commented.

"They sure do!" I laughed.

"But," Charlie wanted to know, "why are we planting flowers in our vegetable garden?"

"Good question," I said as I rumpled his dark hair.

"The marigolds will keep the bean beetles from spoiling our vegetables," I told him.

Taking his hand, I showed him how to poke small finger holes here and there along the row of beans.

"Only this deep." I said, holding his thumb against his finger. "If the seeds are buried too deeply they won't grow, and we need marigold soldiers to protect our garden."

After the marigolds were planted, Charlie and I stood together quietly looking at our garden. In my eyes, it was full of vegetables and as good as harvested. Charlie saw nothing but dirt.

Every day he looked for some sign that the beans were growing. By the end of the week, he'd become discouraged. "Maybe the beans won't grow," he said one morning.

"I'll bet they're growing right now!" I said. Pulling on my old red sweater, I hurried toward the garden.

Charlie followed with dragging steps.

I stooped down and carefully picked at the dirt near the end of the fence. Soon I'd uncovered a sprouted bean and laid it in Charlie's hand. His eyes grew bright with new excitement.

He showed it to Tom.

"Wow!" said Tom, hooking his thumbs through his belt.

He showed it to Steven.

"Hmmm," said Steven, raising one eyebrow.

Tom wanted to show it to Arnie.

Steven wanted to show it to Paul.

Charlie wanted to show it to everyone.

By the end of the second week, tiny green-bean plants were peeking out of the earth. They stood in a straight row along the edge of the rusty wire fence. I showed Charlie how to curl the tender vines around the wire to help them climb the fence.

The lacy green foliage of the marigold army had also grown up. I showed Charlie how to thin the plants.

"Pinch off the plants that don't get off to a good start," I said. "Thinning is important, it helps the healthy plants get the food and water they need."

One day, Charlie noticed the bean buds. Soon the buds opened and the pale pink petals of the bean blossoms unfolded. Busy bees and butterflies visited the garden.

"Don't frighten the bees," Charlie warned Steven. "They're pollinating the vegetables."

Together they watched a fuzzy bee buzz from one flower to another as it gathered nectar to take back to the hive.

When I hoed between the rows, Charlie pulled weeds. He was careful not to disturb the vegetable roots. Steven and Tom helped keep the garden watered when it didn't rain.

Soon, thin velvety beans hung on the strong vines. Charlie watched them grow long and thick. When they were about as big as my finger, I said, "Okay, Charlie, let's pick beans!"

"Can I help?" asked Tom.

"Sure," said Charlie. He showed Tom how to hold the vine with one hand and pluck the bean off with the other. "If you pull them like this," he explained, "you won't hurt the vines."

Soon I was cooking beans for supper three times a week and canning several pints a day.

The boys picked beans for Grandma Arey, too.

"What lovely beans," she commented. "Where did you get them?

"Charlie raised them," Steven told her. "He's a bean expert."

Soon Grandma's freezer was full of beans.

Charlie picked beans every day and the beans kept growing.

The neighborhood children noticed the beans, too. Charlie picked beans for them to take home.

Charlie was getting pretty tired of beans when an early frost brought the harvest to an end.

But now it was time for football.

Steven said, "We need someone to hold the ball when we kick."

Raising one eyebrow, Charlie said, "I can do that."

Tom said, "We need a referee."

The little bean expert hooked his thumbs over his belt and said, "I can do that, too."

Alpha

NO ONE in Pointless could read or write or tell a tale.

The old ones had known these things. But on a certain day in the long ago, a powerful leader had decreed reading a crime, writing a corruption and telling tales a treachery. So it was that two generations of common people had never seen a book, written a letter or heard a story told.

However, while the common people were illiterate, the leaders of this isolated village continued to read and write and post decrees. At the post stood a crier who memorized decrees and shouted newly established laws to passersby.

In this village lived a crone the people called "Alpha-the-mute." She was very old and never spoke. She remembered the day the books were burned in the village square, and her father's voice still rang in her ears.

"No!" he'd shouted, sealing his fate. "I will not conform to unjust law!"

So the authorities ordered him flogged because he'd written a story and refused to surrender his manuscript. Then the law enforcers tied him upright in a wooden cart and drove him through the streets. He died somewhere along the way and his lifeless body was returned to his family that night.

In the morning his frightened wife took the forbidden manuscript to the authorities and it was burned in the public square, which was known as the civil commons. So it was that little Alpha saw the fire in her father's words and watched them burn to ash.

When the enforcers left, Alpha knelt, crossed her body with a pagan sign and filled her handkerchief with the soft warm ash of her father's words. Carefully she rolled them into a bundle and carried them home.

"Papa," she vowed softly, "I won't let them forget."

These had been her final words. For she'd never spoken again.

Now Alpha was old and bent, and her steps were slow and labored. But she went to the commons every day. She went alone. She sat alone. She left alone. She never spoke. For some reason, her muteness annoyed the authorities. They didn't know why, but they found her silence extremely uncomfortable. So they watched her carefully, hoping to find her engaged in some offensive conduct.

But they could not discover Alpha breaking any Pointless law. Therefore, they could not prevent her daily ritual of occupying the commons. It irritated the authorities that she sat in the very place where the books had been burned so long ago.

The old woman particularly offended one of the enforcers. His great-grandfather had been among those who had beaten Alpha's father, watched him die and left his bloody body at the widow's door. Many times his great-grandfather had told his son how the man had refused to surrender his manuscript. Then the son told his son. Therefore, the sons had grown to despise the memory of the vile rebel who'd broken the law and resisted the enforcers.

So it was that Vikre paid particular attention to Alpha. He often followed her from the commons, through the streets. She always took the same route. It was the way the cart had taken her dying father for his final humiliation before the Pointless population.

The man hated the stumbling steps of the old woman. He hated her eyes, her hands and her bent frame.

"I should kill her," he thought. "No one would care."

So one rainy night he crept to Alpha's window, determined to put an end to her silent reproach. He watched her light a candle. He saw her take a tattered bundle from a rusty tin, hold it to her bosom and weep.

Perhaps it was the old woman's tears that put an end to his unreasonable contempt. Perhaps the cold rain took the heat from his murderous passion. I only know that he retreated in sodden boots and never came to Alpha's window again.

After Vikre's departure, Alpha got up and went to the corner cupboard. She returned with a large copper plate and polished it with the corner of her long white apron. Then she placed it on the table where her father had written the forbidden manuscript. She could almost see him leaning over his papers, almost smell the ink and hear the hurried scratch of the quill.

At last she opened the bundle and sprinkled the contents onto the gleaming copper plate. Then in the yellow light of the flickering candle, she watched entranced as the ashes began to form themselves into letters, words and sentences.

"No one in Pointless could read, or write, or tell a tale..." it began.

She read quickly, and as she progressed down through the paragraphs, the ashes arranged themselves into new sentences. Each time she came to the end, she raised her eyes to the top and found new words. She stopped frequently to rest her eyes. Then she'd wipe away her tears and read on.

At last she poured the ashes back into the little bundle, returned it to the tin and snuffed out the candle.

Little Medicine Drum Lake

MAGGIE RED HAWK JACKSON had been sick for several weeks and it was time for her family to go to the agency to pick up their reservation food rations.

Although the Indian agent would insist that Maggie be present for food distribution, her husband felt otherwise.

"No," Joe had told her. "I'll take the little ones, but you're too sick to travel. It will be a rough ride in the wagon and if it should rain..."

Although Maggie understood his concern, she was troubled to think they would probably be denied their full rations simply because she was unable to travel.

She watched the eager children pack for the journey. They rolled their blankets around a bundle of extra clothes, tied it with a leather strap and dragged it to the door.

Joe boiled several potatoes, brewed a pot of tea and filled the pail with fresh water. He put all this on a small table near Maggie's bed and placed the slop bucket nearby. Then he filled the kerosene lamp.

"Is there anything else I can get for you?" he asked.

"My sewing basket and Little Joe's shirt," she said.

Before leaving, Joe put the children on the bed and they held each other for a long time. "We'll be back in two sleeps," he said.

"Goodbye, Little Joe," Maggie whispered into the tousled black hair of her four-year-old son.

"Take care of your little brother," she told Katie.

"I will, Mama," the six-year-old promised.

This particular daughter would soon be taken from her family and sent to a distant Indian residential school. It was something Maggie tried not to think about. But she held Katie extra tight—and extra long.

At last the door was closed between them and Maggie was alone. She listened to the wagon creak and groan as it went up the hill. She heard Joe's gentle voice urging the old horses along.

Then Maggie drank a little tea and went to sleep. She woke up as the sun set. Through the window she could see the rosy sky reflected on the quiet water of the lake.

When it was dark, she scratched a match on the wall and watched it sputter into a brief but fiery life. Carefully she lit the lamp and laid back to rest.

Then she picked up Little Joe's shirt, held it against her face and smelled his sweetness.

Maggie knew she was dreadfully ill and wondered if her family would return to find that she'd passed over while they were gone. It wasn't that she feared the passing but, like any mother, she wanted to be there for her children during the difficult years that lay before them.

Tears were streaming down her gaunt face when she heard a knock on the door.

"Come in," she called, quickly wiping her eyes with the small soiled shirt.

The door opened slowly and a tall elder man stepped into the warm glow of lamplight that filled the one-room log cabin.

"Welcome, welcome," she said. "I'm sorry I can't get up. There's food. Take what you need. Please, help yourself."

The man ate a piece of cold fish and a potato. Then he pulled a chair close to the bed.

He filled two cups with tea and sat down. Maggie found that she was too weak to raise the cup to her lips.

The man held the cup for her.

"You're very sick," he said softly.

Maggie nodded.

"Creator has sent me to help you," the man told her. "I will stay with you tonight and tell you stories."

The man accompanied his words with the voice of a small medicine drum. Soon the exhausted woman had fallen asleep but the sound of the drum filled her dreams. She opened her eyes to find that he was still at her side. The sunlight of another day was spilling through the window. The cabin was warm.

The man leaned over her and smiled. "Feeling better?" he asked, as he offered her a bowl of hot wild rice cereal.

"Yes, thank you," Maggie said.

With some assistance she was able to sit up. Then taking the bowl, she ate hungrily.

The man picked up the drum and told another story. Later he prepared a light mid-day meal and washed the dishes.

The day went so fast that Maggie was surprised when she saw the bright sunset lighting the water in front of the house.

"I'm going to live," she said. "I'm going to raise my children. I'm going to get well and strong again!"

"You're going to live," the man repeated. "But you won't be quite as you were before. Your legs will never be strong and you will require help to get up and down. When your children are grown, they will carry you."

"No!" Maggie cried. "I don't want to be a burden to my good husband and my dear children. I'd rather leave now!"

"Your family will never consider you a burden," he promised. "They will carry you without complaint."

Then the man began to drum and sing. Healing power washed over Maggie and without lighting the lamp, she fell asleep.

In the morning he gave her meat. She wondered where he'd gotten the venison but didn't ask. "Perhaps he took a deer without the agent's consent," she thought.

She ate meat at mid-day, too. "I feel so much better," she told him. "Surely you're mistaken about my legs."

But the man shook his head and closing his eyes he said, "I see your husband is returning. Soon I must leave. I'll sing once more—your healing song."

Afterwards he stood and walked to the door. He turned once and smiled, and then—he was gone.

Within minutes she heard the wagon coming.

She was sitting up when Joe opened the door and cautiously peeked toward the bed. Suddenly he was beside her!

The children rushed in behind him. They spoke excitedly about their journey, filling the little house with laughter.

With tears in his eyes Joe confessed, "I was afraid I'd find you dead."

"A man came with a medicine drum. He took care of me. He told stories. He sang my healing song," said Maggie.

"But there are no tracks on the road," Joe puzzled.

"He was here," Maggie insisted.

Joe walked around the house several times before he saw the tracks of a man coming from the lake—and returning to the lake.

"He came in a canoe," Joe decided.

But when he examined the lakeshore where the man came out of the water, there was no sign of a canoe being dragged up on the sand.

"A spirit has been with you," he told Maggie later.

Maggie sighed, "He was like a man."

Maggie regained her health. But, just as the man had said, her legs remained weak. Her husband had to lift her in and out of the wagon.

When her husband grew old, her children carried her.

They never complained and never made her feel that she was a burden. "We want to make your life easier," they told her.

Over the years many people came to hear Maggie tell the story of the healing spirit who had given her the time she needed to raise her children.

Joe would lead visitors to the lake and show them where the tracks had come out of the water.

Although the man was never seen again, Maggie's story has become an inspiration to many.

After Joe passed over, Maggie began selling her land. But her children cared for her and she was able to remain in her cabin on Little Medicine Drum Lake until her death in 1942.

Eventually even this land was sold to a white family who wanted to build a summer home on the lakeshore. In the course of "improving" their land, they tore down the cabin. Only the floor remained for several years. Then it was bulldozed into a heap, burned and forgotten.

Sugar Bush Journal

I REMEMBER the crusty snow crunching under our boots as we broke trail into the sugar bush. I remember that the cooking scaffold looked like a lonely skeleton with its arms flung out in welcome.

Like a grid, the scaffold shadow marked the place where we would build the fire. Digging down through the snow and matted leaves, we prepared a fireplace on the rich, dark forest soil. The children had already gathered bundles of dry sticks which they wigwammed over bits of paper and birch bark. The wigwam was lit on the wind-blown side and fed with larger sticks until a brisk blaze was leaping toward the sky.

Because we had no buildings there, at the end of the past sugaring season we had stacked our inverted catch-cans and cooking pails near the scaffold and covered them with tarpaper held in place with heavy poles. Each year when we arrived, we dug them out, filled the pails with fresh snow, and hung them from the scaffold with strong wires. The fire licked eagerly at the black pails as we added more snow, until we had enough hot water to wash and rinse 300 catch-cans.

I have an especially vivid memory of felling a large dead maple. To our dismay, we discovered it had been home to several flying squirrels. We watched them glide down among the trees to seek new hiding places. It's quite unusual to see them during the day. In that short time we probably saw more than most people will see in a lifetime.

As the men cut and split the wood, the women and children hauled it to the camp on a long toboggan. There, they stacked it like a log cabin fortress wall around the scaffold. The wall of wood would serve as a windbreak near the fire, where the logs would dry quickly if it should rain or snow. It took several days to get the wood ready. We knew there would be little time for gathering wood when the sap began to run.

When we had stacked enough wood, we went home to wait.

I watched the box elders near our home because we know that when the box elders begin to weep, it's time to tap the maples.

In late winter, the sap rises up into the trees to begin another season of growth. The fluctuating temperatures of cold, freezing nights followed by warm, thawing days trigger the process.

How anxious we became as the days passed. At last we saw bright tears glistening in the branches of the box elders. The sap was running!

We returned to camp with a brace and bit, and a box of clean taps. The children distributed catch-cans. We tapped the small trees once on the sunrise side, so they would begin to flow early in the day. Larger trees would produce more sap, so we could tap them more than once. One great tree held five cans, well spaced around its huge trunk. We called that tree "Grandfather."

We stood together to witness the tapping of the first tree. As we turned the bit, a long curl of moist wood appeared. Then we removed the bit, placed a spout in the hole and quickly hung a can place. We watched a drop of sap appear, glitter in the sunlight, fall from the spout and splash into the bottom of the can with a musical "ting." With that drop, another harvest had begun!

Because the sweet-tasting sap is only about three percent sugar, it may take more than 30 gallons of sap to produce one gallon of syrup. Boiling the sap to make syrup is long, hard work.

But although the sugar bush is a place of intense work, it is also a place of spiritual renewal and personal enrichment. It's hard to imagine a better place to be in March.

If I got to camp early, I'd find the sap still frozen in the spouts. I'd lay wood for a large fire, about eight feet long and three feet wide, fill the cooking pails with sap from the storage barrels and hang the pails over the fire. Then I'd brew a pot of sap-coffee.

As the sun climbed into the sky, the grove began to warm and I'd walk away from the snapping fire to listen to the sap song. I'd hear it begin far away. Ting. The sap had thawed. Ting. It fell into waiting catch-cans. Ting. Ting. Soon I was surrounded by the happy rhythm. But as the cans began to fill, the song subsided, for only empty cans sing.

Sometimes I thought, "If we didn't come to release the maple sap, life would not return to the land. For life flows from this grove into all the world."

Although the sugar bush enriched my life with quiet memories, it would never be complete without the laughter of happy children.

The children spent many hours swinging in the arms of an ancient maple broken by storms and years. The giant seemed unwilling to resign itself to the earth and, propped up on huge limbs it invited the children to many adventures. They called it "the love tree," because they loved to play there.

The children also learned to be comfortable with small wild things. Near the camp, two ospreys made their summer home. Their ragged-looking nest clung to the top of a dead poplar. How eagerly we welcomed their return from the south, as they circled our camp like great winged sentinels!

The staccato of hungry woodpeckers often broke the quiet of the warming days. Squirrels and later chipmunks visited us for handouts and flicked their tails in thanks for our generosity.

One year, two playful weasels came to live in our wood stack and made us laugh with their favorite game. They chased each other through the stack and suddenly popped up between the wood sticks. Then, almost before we saw them leave, they blinked at us from somewhere else. They went so fast that it was like watching six weasels running around in the woodpile!

In the evenings we sat together in the glow of the fire, lost in private worlds of thought. But as the darkness gathered, it seemed to draw us nearer to each other. Around the campfire, we knit families and sealed friendships.

Each night, we carried our precious burden of steaming syrup home.

Walking down the trail, I felt close to the people who came to the grove long ago. I could almost see them walking among the trees, peering into catch-cans and nodding in satisfaction. I could almost hear the mud sucking softly at their feet, as they went to warm themselves at our abandoned fire still glowing with bright coals.

We celebrated the closing of the sugar bush with a thanksgiving feast. Then, one by one, we picked up our packs to leave. Single file, we moved down the muddy trail. One by one, we paused at the turn in the path to look back.

The quiet woods, the crisp spring air, the cry of the owl, and the echo of tradition had had its way with us and we promised to return again, when the box elders began to weep.

Sweet Smoky Blues

I'D BEEN CHARGED with watching the maple syrup cooker so it wouldn't boil over. There were also three barrels of sap bubbling the steam away. Annie and Laura had just returned from emptying sap so the holding barrel was full.

After returning to camp, Annie began splitting wood while Laura renewed the fire. I was quick to see and eliminate a brief but intense flare. Using a long pole, I scattered the flaming wood to cool the fire.

Earlier that day I'd noticed that the sparks clung to the shelter roof and didn't die out as quickly as I thought they should. I also noted that the fire was swirling rather violently. But with several sugar bush veterans in camp, I decided it was not going to be a problem. In fact, I told Laura that the fire had learned a new dance. She smiled and glanced into the flames but said nothing. When she went out to stack the woodpile I was alone with the fire.

Soon I smelled plastic burning. I checked my boots then stepped out to tell Annie and Laura to check their boots, too. When I reentered the shelter I was hit by a terrible odor. Then the roof burst into flames. Burning tarpaper and melted plastic began falling into our boiling barrels. I shouted, "Fire!" and we flew into action. We formed an instant bucket brigade with Annie climbing to the roof while Laura and I passed sap from the holding barrel.

Then I went inside and began throwing cans of sap against the inside of the roof. After many desperate minutes we got the blaze under control but there was a great loss of syrup and sap, not to mention the gaping hole in the roof.

On Easter Sunday we had a big dinner and an egg hunt at the camp and the fire seemed forgotten. However, Annie was later presented with a book of spent matches. The award was given in recognition of her being the camp supervisor at the time of the fire.

It was soon decided that we would close down camp because we had all the syrup we needed for the coming year. Usually we close camp when the maple buds are as big as squirrel ears.

We began pulling taps and bagging catch cans. The cookers and holding barrel were still full. Some of the men said they would finish cooking the remaining sap and the resulting syrup would be given to some of our hard-working helpers.

We had opened the camp with a naming ceremony, giveaway and feast. Now we were closing the camp with a family dinner.

I watched the smoke drift away through the trees and listened to the voices around me but I heard no words at all. I was only aware of a certain contentment that hummed about me. Closing my eyes, I felt like a fetus who had been carried into the sugar bush camp within her mother's womb.

When I opened my eyes, I looked up through the bare branches and thanked Creator for another happy gathering. I asked that I be allowed to return to the sugar bush next year and enjoy the sweet smoky blues without another unexpected fire and another hole in the roof.

Sugar Bush Easter

OUR FAMILY has a traditional Easter feast at the sugar bush camp every year. But this year I would be going on my new titanium knee. I didn't know how it would function over the rough terrain. Cedar and I walked into the bush and were met by my grandson Brendan on the four-wheeler. We accepted a ride to the campsite. Then he returned to the parking area for food and other passengers.

I had brought a small hand-painted rabbit to hang in the sugar shack. I'd made salt/flour dough, baked it in a slow oven and painted it yellow. I'd also decorated a sturdy basket for the centerpiece. Missy and Avie filled it with donuts and it was soon emptied. Afterwards I gave the basket to Chey for her birthday.

Eventually there was a good crowd of family and friends gathered around the smoky fire. Four generations of my family was represented. I had five children present, nine grandchildren and one great-grandchild in the group. Daughter Esther was carrying one more grandchild in her womb. Although my son Charles was not physically present I could feel him thinking of us all the way from Hayward, Wisconsin.

Of course, there was too much food. The menu included venison, fish, ham, wild rice, frybread, blueberries, strawberries, potatoes, coffee, elderberry tea and several cakes. Food was reheated over the campfire or on the Coleman stove. Juices and carbonated beverages were kept cold in a pile of icy snow.

Annie prepared a spirit dish and her father prayed.

After dinner all the strong young people started carrying wood and piling it around the shack to create a windbreak. Soon one wall was up and two more were begun. Two low slab tables were built where the little ones could rest. Ceila inaugurated the first and was soon bundled up in a sleeping bag for a midday nap.

During the brief but frequent intervals of silence I listened to the wind playing those old harp songs in the treetops.

As I sat in the midst of wind songs, laughter and stories, I remembered old camps, old friends and departed loved ones. I also remembered one Easter with my sister Shirley and our parents at Berg's logging camp. I don't remember the exact location but it was here in northern Minnesota.

Mama had cut paper sacks into narrow strips and woven two small baskets. Then she gathered some long grass, made two nests and tucked one into each basket. Before we went to bed that night we placed the baskets near the door. Mama said the Easter bunny would find them and leave gifts for two good girls.

Soon she was tucking us into bed. We slept in the top bunk. Our parents had a full bed below. There was a curtain around the bed, which she closed.

Then I heard some unusual activity in the kitchen end of the small shack. So I put my eye to a tiny hole and saw Mama engaged in the process of coloring boiled eggs. Perhaps she heard me gasp for she hurried to the bed and rearranged the curtain. I could no longer see through the hole so I went to sleep.

Early the next day we saw that the Easter bunny had indeed found and filled our baskets. Inside each basket were three colored eggs. They were red and blue and yellow. I kept the blue one in my basket for several days because it was so beautiful.

When it was time to leave our sugar camp, grandson Saige took Cedar and me back to the road on the four-wheeler. As we roared along, I remembered how we struggled up and down the muddy trails carrying tools, wood, food, children and syrup. Today, modern motorized vehicles make the work easier but rupture the silence and taint the air with exhaust fumes.

When these children look back, their memories of sugar bush will not be the same as those that bless and enrich my journey. But the end result—maple sugar and syrup—remain unaltered and savored from one generation to the next.

Sugar Bush Voices

THOSE WHO GATHER maple sap can name the signs that tell them when it's time to tap the trees. Many will say the sap begins to rise when warm days are followed by cold nights. This is true and this we know.

But I prefer the sign my mother waited for. She used to tell me, "When the box elders begin to weep, it's time to tap the maples."

So I spent much time looking up into the branches of the tall box elders that surrounded our old house. Sometimes I would listen for weeping in the night but Mama said they wept in the warmth of the afternoon. Then one day it happened that a box elder tear fell upon my upturned face and I knew that what she said was true. The box elders were weeping.

So many years later, when we drove to the sugar bush camp and parked the car at the end of the tar I was keenly aware of the privilege I had of entering this small but rich domain. Once again I was greeted by sugar bush voices.

The great white pine reached high into the April sky, poised and waiting for the wind. One after another they joined their voices as the song moved from tree to tree. I raised my hands and touched the sighing breath around me before stepping off toward the camp. As my boots crushed the snow beneath each step, new and unique voices rose around my feet. It takes many steps to reach the camp and the icy song enriched my journey.

Everyone was out emptying catch cans when I arrived so I was alone with the fire. I put a sprig of cedar on the coals for a symbolic cleansing and washed my hands in the smoke. The excited voices of the flaming tongues offered their fiery poems.

Later I took a bucket and went out among the trees. I put down a bit of tobacco and thanked Creator for the generous gift of nourishing sap. Then I emptied a can into a bucket, re-hung the can and heard the metal ring as the sap drops fell into the can. After emptying and re-hanging several cans I held my breath and listened to this sweetly ringing song of life. When all the cans were emptied we returned to camp and our varied voices joined the chorus.

The crackling fire had to be fed. So someone began splitting wood. The boiling sap sizzled, bubbled and hissed. Of course, these lyrical voices were also blended into the sugar bush symphony.

The shouts and laughter of playful children punctuated the great song.

Then a weary child was lifted into the blanket swing and the rope squeaked against the bark of the supporting trees. A grandmother sang a soft lullaby and leaned into the swing to kiss the little one. The child smiled once, her eyelids fluttered and closed.

When the sap had boiled down to thin syrup it was poured into a clean bucket, covered with a dishtowel and carried back to the road. After the warm dry day, the snow had melted. Now the boots made sucking sounds as we followed one another through the mud. A nation of small birds flew over us and their raspy songs trailed behind them.

As we left with the precious gift of maple syrup, I listened to the voices of the ancestors whispering around us. They said that even in the midst of great and widespread change, the sugar bush voices remain the same.

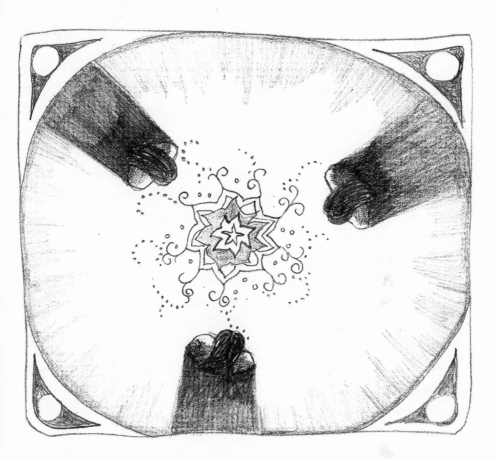

Keeper of the Hair Bowl

GRANDMOTHER DIED suddenly, as so many had during those difficult days. For that reason, her eldest granddaughter began to clean the old woman's small tar-papered house by the big lake.

If Grandmother had sold the valuable lakeshore property she would have been a rich woman. But she'd held on to the land so she could leave something for her surviving children. Eventually, however, the land had been divided and, bit by bit, it would be lost.

But today her orphaned granddaughter, Rose, would discover an old mystery carefully wrapped and packed in the bottom of a wooden barrel. The barrel was full of rug rags, colorful yarn and remnants of fabrics the old woman had been saving for quilts.

So it was that Rose found herself holding an exquisite bowl. After turning it around several times to admire the shape and design, she looked inside. She was startled to find a long braid of human hair coiled in the bottom of the bowl. It was an old braid from an old person. The braid had been tied at the ends with faded red ribbons. Rose wondered whose hair it was and what her obligations were now that she had become the keeper of the hair bowl.

Thoughtfully she put the bowl and its mysterious contents into a box of things she would keep for herself. Then she went on sorting the rags and folding the fabrics in neat stacks for the giveaway, which would celebrate Grandmother's life one year from the day of her death.

After the four-day wake and burial, Rose turned her attention to the hair bowl. She fully recognized her responsibility to the hair and decided to seek counsel on the matter.

On a bright spring morning Rose made a bundle of several carefully chosen items from Grandmother's possessions, put the hair bowl in a bag and went to visit Maggie Sore Eyes.

After a warm greeting followed by three cups of maple-sweetened wild mint tea and four fig cookies, Rose placed the bundle on the table between them. Maggie opened the bundle and found a tin of tobacco, a pair of blanket skippers, an embroidered apron and three skeins of yarn. She smiled at Rose and thanked her.

When the gift had been accepted, Rose showed her the hair bowl. The elder woman lifted the braid and held it in her hands for several long minutes. Then she laid the hair on the table, opened a nearby chest and removed several items.

She placed a large abalone shell, a bundle of sage and a sweetgrass braid on the table. Prayerfully she prepared and lit a cleansing smudge. The women sat together in silence as the shadows of the tall trees crept across the yard.

At last Maggie spoke. "We will be visited in our dreams. After you dream, you must come to me with the hair bowl. I will be waiting for my dream, too. When we receive instructions we will know what we must do."

Rose was greatly relieved as she walked home late that afternoon.

That night she had her dream. An elder woman, whom she'd never seen before, came to her and said she wanted to give her a gift. Reaching up, the elder cut off one of her braids with a stone blade and held it out to Rose.

When she woke up she dressed quickly and hurried to Maggie's small house. After sipping a cup of hot coffee, Rose told her dream. The elder woman listened then told her dream to Rose.

Maggie lit the smudge. Together the women prayed for guidance and understanding. Afterwards, they discussed what must be done. They decided to create a ceremony of compassion, burn the hair in a nearby balsam grove and wait.

It took several days to gather everything they needed for the ceremony. When all was ready they went to the grove, performed the ceremony and waited. At last, another woman joined them. Rose recognized her as the woman in her dream. Her braid had been restored and she was pleased. Now she could continue her journey.

For many years Rose kept her own hair in the bowl. She burned the hair under a full moon several times a year.

Eventually she became the mother of several children and her eldest son was married. Tanya, the young bride, was interested in the ceremonies of women.

But before the newlyweds could celebrate their first anniversary, Tanya became ill and Rose prepared a cleansing ceremony for her healing. She also decided to give Tanya the hair bowl. So she presented the gift with a braid of sweet grass inside. Tanya looked into the bowl for a long time. Then she said, "I must tell you my dream."

The young woman spoke softly: "An elder woman came to me. She said she wanted to give me a gift. Then reaching up, she cut off one of her braids and held it out to me."

Rose was overcome with emotion and turned toward the window to hide her feelings. Then it was that she saw four women standing in the yard. They were her mother, her grandmother, Maggie and the elder woman she had seen in the balsam grove so many years before. The women smiled at Rose, then looked beyond her at Tanya who smiled back. Slowly the four women faded into another dimension and were gone.

Tanya reached across the table to hold Rose's hand. They sat together in the gathering darkness and thanked the visitors for coming.

Sharing the same dream would enrich their long relationship. The women would enjoy several good years together and many times they would be asked to make ceremonies for the healing, cleansing and guidance of other women and their children.

Big Sam

B IG SAM was a lumberjack. He was six-foot-four and had never asked for help. He didn't expect it, either. In fact, he didn't want it.

He'd been a large child, too; often challenged by older boys and beaten by adults who looked upon his size as a measure of his maturity and experience.

Although he was tall and strong, he wasn't particularly attractive and was shy around women. He was nearly forty when he met Mary at a Wisconsin powwow in 1962. She was half his age, with quiet eyes and graceful steps. He enjoyed her soft voice and easy laughter. She needed freedom and security. She found that with him.

Although he went back to Minnesota alone, he returned the following weekend. Mary was waiting. Her bags were packed and she was ready to go. A month later they were married in the Episcopal Church on his reservation.

She got a housekeeping position at the Indian Health Service Hospital and he continued cutting logs for the Wilson brothers.

He thought he'd never tire of the way she looked up at him with those quiet brown eyes or the way she felt when he held her slender body in his big arms. For a long time that was enough. But after a few years, he'd become disappointed because they had no children. It was unlike any disappointment he'd ever experienced. It was a big, deep empty ache that found a home in him and never went away.

At first he wondered what was wrong with her. Why didn't she get pregnant and bless him with children? Then they talked to a doctor and they were both tested. The doctor told them there was no reason why Mary could not conceive. He said the problem was Sam's low sperm count.

After that the ache got bigger and went deeper. It was so big it filled Sam's waking hours and visited his dreams. It was too deep to touch and too empty to fill. It changed the way he felt about Mary.

When he'd thought it was her fault they'd remained childless, he accepted her failure and did what he could to shield her from self-reproach.

But afterwards he began to argue with her. He often shouted at her and complained about the way she cooked, the way she laughed, the way she sang. So she pulled away from him and he didn't like that either. The more he needed her, the more she wasn't there for him.

But then he began seeing a young widow in a nearby village. He liked the bold way Susan looked up at him and how she leaned against him when they said, "Good-bye."

She didn't know about the low sperm count. She could assume that he had no children because his wife was barren.

Susan opened his shirt and slipped her arms around him, "Why don't you have any big sons to cut wood for your wife?"

They laughed together when he said, "Because Mary's uterus is as big as a pumpkin and as dry as a gourd!"

They'd been seeing each other for about six months when Susan told him she was pregnant. He gave a hoot, picked her up and twirled her around the room. Now he would be a father! Now he would have a son.

But what about Mary? Would she stand in the way of his happiness? Would she allow him a divorce or would she cling to him? He wrestled with the question for several days. In the end it was Susan who went to speak with Mary.

Afterwards Sam went home and found his wife sitting in a dark house.

"You can go," she said. "I've packed your clothes. Take your guns and power saw. But there will be no divorce. I know Susan wants you now but I don't think it will last long. When it's over, you can come back, if you wish. But when you return, you must enlarge the house so you can have your own room."

Sam went away.

He moved in with Susan and it was wonderful. Susan treated him like gold. She made him feel young and strong and virile again. He held her pregnant body close and dreamed of the son they would have. At last the big, deep, empty ache was gone. But after several weeks, Susan resumed her moon time. Sam took her to a doctor in another town.

"What went wrong?" Sam wanted to know.

The young doctor shrugged, "It happens."

Sam knew that Susan wouldn't become pregnant again. At least not while she was with him. The ache returned and he began to mistreat her. So she began to shrink from him and he despised her for it. She didn't want him anymore and he didn't want her either.

He wasn't surprised when he got to her house one night and discovered his clothes and guns on the porch. He began sleeping in his truck. He cut logs all day and ate at the café. He knew he could return to share the house with Mary. But it wouldn't be like going home. So he rented a cheap room at the Boston Hotel.

One autumn afternoon he got his pick-up stuck axle-deep in a muddy rut. As he tried to push it out, a crushing pain wrapped itself around his chest and pulled him down into a soft dark hole.

When he opened his eyes a woman was staring into his face. "He's awake," she said.

Slowly he began to realize that he was in the hospital. He could see someone sitting beside the bed. When he was able to focus his eyes, he saw that it was Mary.

"I want you to get well," she said. "I want you to come home."

He couldn't trust himself to speak, so he nodded his head.

After several days of bed rest, he was released and went home with Mary. She took two weeks off work to be with him while he recuperated.

He felt shy and childish in her care. He felt awkward and useless, too.

She'd put a small, comfortable bed in the living room for him and a spoon in a clean mayonnaise jar on his bedside table.

"When you need help," she told him, "shake the jar."

But she was so alert to his needs that he didn't need the "bell." She was attentive, friendly, gentle and kind. He was cheerful and talkative during the day, but he often wept at night. He remembered how he'd mistreated Mary. How he'd betrayed her trust for a younger woman, and ridiculed her to hide his own shortcomings.

In the spring he was strong enough to work in the yard, and Mary told him to begin enlarging the house.

"We can hire someone to help you," she said.

So he made a plan, purchased building supplies and hired his brother. It wasn't long before the floor was down and the walls were up. Then the roof was completed and the windows and doors were installed.

Sam could see how much Mary liked the well-lit room, so he offered to let her have it.

"I'll take the old room," he said and watched a happy smile spread slowly over her face.

She moved her things into the new room immediately. Sam's cot and table went into the room that had once been their honeymoon love nest. Then she hung his clothes neatly in the small closet and hurried from the room.

Later she hummed as she washed dishes. Then she sat down to crochet a lace edge on an embroidered tablecloth she was making for one of her sisters. Sam was happy as he sat in his old chair reading. But when Mary went into her room and closed the door softly behind her, he dropped the paper on the floor and felt a sudden ache growing inside him. Soon it was bigger than any pain he'd ever known. He sat for a long time staring at the light under Mary's door.

After five years, the ache was nearly forgotten. He'd become comfortable with their living arrangement and greatly enjoyed Mary's pleasant companionship.

During the early years of their marriage they'd gone to Wisconsin a few times to visit Mary's five sisters. Now their visits became more frequent. All the girls had children and some of them even had grandchildren. It was during these visits that Sam watched Mary hold those warm, brown babies and gaze upon their innocent beauty. He listened as she sang those old rocking-chair-songs that women keep for the little ones. He watched her play games with the children. She told them stories, too.

He saw the older nieces and nephews come to her for counsel. He heard her share personal stories to comfort and encourage them as they struggled to find their way in this world.

Then one day he was called to the hospital. Mary had collapsed at work. "Hurry!"

By the time he got there, she was gone.

He couldn't believe it. "No! No!"

He called her sisters. "Mary's dead."

"No! No!"

It was after the funeral when her sister Clara came to Sam with several large bundles.

"I found them in her closet," she said. "If you don't want them, I'll take them home. But I think you should see this."

Slowly he opened a bundle. Inside he found dozens of yellowing hand-hemmed white flannel diapers, several cans of sweet-smelling powder and a small quilt. In another there were neatly folded baby jackets and gowns adorned with tiny embroidered flowers, butterflies and birds. He took the quilt and pushed the bundles toward Clara.

"Take them," he whispered hoarsely.

When Clara left the room, he gathered the quilt in his big hands and covered his face with the pale fabric. He could smell Mary in the folds and he wept until he was sick.

Several days later he found himself at her grave. The good smelling earth was piled high and covered with wilted flowers. He spread the quilt on the ground and sat down.

"Mary," he asked softly, "why didn't you tell me? We could have talked about our disappointment. Instead, I let it turn to anger while you lived alone in your sorrow. We could have shared the heartache. But I let it get big and deep and empty. I know it's too late, Mary. But I'm so goddamn sorry."

Six months later Sam followed Mary to the other side, and Clara took the little quilt back to Wisconsin. Before winter, one of her daughters was wrapping a baby in the old quilt. The child was named Mary, in memory of a dear, but lonely auntie, buried on a reservation in northern Minnesota.

Dream Drum

THE JOURNEY had begun from a small village beyond the Arctic Circle in northern Canada. It began with a fourteen-inch black ash hoop, not easily secured above the tree line. It had been a gift from a relative who lived in a warmer land. Then a piece of rawhide had been stretched over the frame, tied and dried. The drum maker always left a bit of caribou hair clinging to the hide. It was his signature. He also made a good drumbeater. He made a drum bag, too.

He'd done all this according to a dream that he'd received under a full moon. He'd heard a prayer that night. The voice had come from far away. It was a female voice asking for a drum. With no more information than that, he'd begun to bring the dream drum into reality.

When it was completed, a man arrived in the village. He was a visitor from Minnesota. He came in a canoe. At once the drum maker recognized him as the one who would carry the drum to its distant destination.

Without hesitation, the drum maker approached the stranger with the request that he take the drum to the woman who was waiting for it. The stranger was surprised, but accepted the commission without question.

Then it was that the woman began to dream about the drum. She saw it coming to her from far away and as she waited she began to make new songs.

After many weeks the man was at her door. She invited him into her house and he handed her the bag with an apology. "I'm sorry, but I lost the beater. It slipped out of the bag and fell into the river. It has been a long journey."

The woman realized that in all her dreams she'd never seen a beater with the drum. So she thanked the man, and gave him a cup of tea, a walleye sandwich and a wedge of blueberry pie. Then he went away. He disappeared into the night like a forgotten dream.

The woman made a good drumbeater and soon she was singing dream songs on the drum and all her songs turned into healing. Mental anguish was her specialty. Although the drum was cleansed before and after every healing, it was soon full of grief. After several years, the drum decided to break. The ash hoop split and the hide tore.

The woman went to an elder and showed her the drum. The elder held the drum for a long time. She listened to the drum and then she said, "This drum wants to go to the other side."

So the woman took the drum back to her house and prayed for guidance. Then she carried the drum into the forest and hung it in a tree. For it was not yet time to send it across.

The drum needed a prolonged period of cleansing. So it hung between earth and sky. It welcomed the seasons and lunar cycles. It embraced rain and snow. It was intimate with squirrels, songbirds and eagles. Frequently nudged by passing deer and sniffed by local bears.

The woman often visited the drum, but never took it home.

The dream drum hung in the tree for several long years.

Then one night, the woman gathered a circle of warrior sisters for ceremony. They would burn the dream drum under a full autumn moon. The spirit of the drum would leave in the smoke.

Far away, in the west of Turtle Island, a young woman was preparing to kill herself. She felt hopelessly worthless and did not want to live through another tearful night and into another lonely day.

But as she prepared to meet her death, the women in Minnesota laid the drum in the ceremonial flames. The desperate woman heard a heartbeat from the sky. She listened to the dream drum song and she was healed. She never heard the sky drum again. But she never gave up on living her life and endured with courage for many years. She died of natural causes at an old age.

The drum dreamer would be lonesome for that drum to the end of her life. But sometimes she heard it singing from the sky and she knew it was waiting for her.

She remembered how she'd nearly refused to accept the drum. She thought the stranger was mistaken. Who would make a drum for her and send it out upon such a journey with no idea where it was going?

But when he told her how the beater had been lost, she recognized it as the drum in her dreams and welcomed it with her whole heart. So they had found each other during the time of her young womanhood and, after a long life, she traveled to the other side where the dream drum welcomed her with new songs.

Frybread Mountain

IT HAPPENED during the summer of 1979 that an elder woman walked from Leech Lake to Lac Courte Oreilles (LCO) in Wisconsin. She carried her belongings in a small backpack and pulled a large wagon heaped with commodity flour, dry milk, salt, shortening and baking powder.

She also brought a large mixing bowl that she'd received from her Uncle TeeDee, a wooden spoon from Cousin Fanny, a long-handled fork from Great-Aunt Rose and a black skillet that had belonged to her own good mother.

The woman came because she had dreamed a mountain and believed that it was her responsibility to see the dream become reality.

When she arrived at LCO she quickly located a likely site, built herself a sturdy wigwam and began to raise the mountain she'd seen in the frosty morning twilight of her winter dream.

She began by mixing great quantities of bread dough and laid it on birch bark mats to rest.

Then she built a stone fire pit, kindled a friendly fire and melted the shortening in her big black skillet. Finally she began forming the frybread and laying it in the hot fat. The oil sizzled around the edges. Soon the dough puffed up beautifully and cooked into perfect pieces of delicious frybread.

When she had cooked enough to fill the wagon she pulled it into the center of the area where the mountain would be located and laid the bread on the ground.

Then she set about the work of making more dough.

Within three days she had exhausted her supply of flour. So she pulled her wagon to the nearest house and asked for more.

The woman of the house, Tilly Tullibee, was reluctant to give her flour to a woman who left bread on the ground. But when she heard the story of the dream and how the elder woman wanted to build a monument to frybread at LCO, Tilly gave her the flour and told her to return for more when it was needed.

So the elder woman was able to continue for a couple more days. But when the gift of flour had been used up, she found her supply of dry milk was also depleted.

When the elder woman returned to Tilly's generous door, Tilly knew it would take more than one source to supply all the flour and dry milk that would be needed to build Frybread Mountain. So she began gathering a volunteer army of women who would join in the dream of building this mountain. They became known as Frybread Sisters Constructors Extraordinaire.

Fire pits multiplied around the site and the mountain grew, at a furious rate as nearly all the women at LCO joined in the effort to bring a dream into reality.

As the mountain grew it became visible to residents at Hayward. Several more women came to join the campaign. They brought their children, too. Some of them built wigwams nearby so they could work at night. It was a beautiful sight!

Well, it wasn't long before Frybread Mountain had been completed.

Now it was time to celebrate!

All the Frybread Sisters prepared food for the event and invited their female relatives from eastern Minnesota and northern Wisconsin to join in the dedication ceremonies.

When the company of women arrived, they dusted themselves with flour, oiled their hair, put on their frybread dresses and climbed up Frybread Mountain.

Then, hand in hand, they danced the lofty heights and were bonded on the greasy slopes.

When the weather got cold, the women carried black plastic trash bags to the top of the mountain. Then they shook them open, stepped inside, pulled the bags up over their butts and sat down. Then with loud screams and excited laughter, they slid to the bottom of Frybread Mountain in their wonderful Frybread Sleds.

Celebrations on Frybread Mountain became traditional events.

Each spring the women gathered at the site to enlarge the mountain. They held annual Sister Frybread Dance Festivals in the summer. There were Frybread Seminars in the fall, and Frybread Sled Parties kept them busy all winter.

Then it happened that the Mother of Frybread Mountain fell ill. Of course, the women wanted to honor her. So she asked that a simple white stone be placed at the foot of the mountain to commemorate her passing. She insisted that they find a stone smaller than her head but larger than her heart. There was to be nothing engraved on it, she said. And so she passed into Frybread Heaven.

Now some of the men began to think that the women were having too much fun and casino revenues had fallen off considerably. An elected official from Washington DeCeit arrived to study the situation and carried a 4,000-page document to the Bureau of Frybread Affairs.

Suspicious that the women were engaged in resistance and eager to crush any possibility of dissent, the Washington officials hired a community of scientists to develop a Frybread Mouse.

After a great deal of taxpayer dollars had been invested in the project, the scientists delivered fourteen mice that could not eat anything but frybread.

Then three top government spies were disguised as Indian women and sent to LCO. They quickly released the mice and returned to the Bureau of Frybread Affairs with a 4,000-page report documenting their success.

It didn't take long for the mice to multiply. Within two months the mountain was gone and the mice, left with nothing more to eat, were dead. It left an awful stink!

The government brought bulldozers from New York and snowplows from Montana. They recruited thirty-six heavy equipment operators from Florida and buried the mice in a local landfill.

So the Great Frybread Mountain has been reduced to a memory and only a few of the Frybread Sisters speak openly of gathering for Frybread Dances.

Sometimes a Sister will shake open a big black trash bag, dust her brow with flour and remember flying down the mountain in her Frybread Sled.

Sometimes, under a Frybread Moon, a lone child will carry a small portion of warm frybread to the old site and leave it on the white stone.

The Tattered Gown

IT HAPPENED when I was in the ninth grade that I was nominated for Cass Lake Homecoming Queen. I really had no enthusiasm for such nonsense, so with my usual grace and dignity, I stood to decline the nomination. How surprised I was to hear myself accepting it instead!

Traditionally, the senior students were crowned and titled. For those of us who remained uncrowned it was an opportunity to dress up and follow the regal red velvet trains of the royal pair in a brief but pompous procession.

Now, being blessed with good common sense, I had no real hope of wearing the crown. However, news of the nomination had reached home before I did.

Previously, no one in my family had ever expected that a funny awkward girl from the poor side of the railroad tracks could receive such a prestigious nomination. But, somehow they had begun to believe that my nomination would undoubtedly be followed by my coronation!

I was amazed at my mother's extreme excitement. "Mama," I warned, "freshmen are never crowned."

But, ignoring my youthful wisdom, she flew through the house looking for a suitable dress for her unaspiring princess. Mama did not understand that I had absolutely no chance of becoming a homecoming queen.

Oh, how I regretted being so foolish as to accept the nomination. Mama would be so disappointed. And what would I wear? I felt myself getting sick.

"Mama," I whispered, "I have been told that I must wear a formal gown."

She was momentarily deflated but not defeated. Mama recruited our relatives. Their mission: find a gown.

But all our relatives were as poor as we and—equally gownless.

However, in the musty, moldy bottom of a forgotten trunk, someone discovered a tattered white floor-length gown. So it was that cousin Margaret's old organdy and voile prom formal was resurrected.

Quickly it was carried to our house and presented to my mother. She shook it vigorously then held it up between us for an appraisal.

I could see that it was nothing more than a glorified rag! I knew it would never be white again.

How awful I would look standing under the bright stage lights with all the well-dressed court attendants. I wondered if I could possibly die before humiliation killed me.

But Mama saw things differently. "This dress is not white," she mused. "This dress is a lovely shade of vanilla cream."

Looking from the gown to Mama and back to the gown again, I saw it through her eyes. "Yes," I agreed, "a lovely shade of vanilla cream."

So the transformation had begun.

We soon discovered that the dress was much too big. So Mama snipped and stitched it to a custom fit.

Mice had chewed holes in the voile overskirt. So Mama cut petals out of a piece of pale pink fabric she found in the rag bag. She embroidered the petals into roses and appliquéd them over the holes. Then she took small artificial flowers and pinned them to the organdy underskirt.

With her keen eye for beauty and her magic silver needle, Mama gave the old dress a whole new identity.

Then she dipped into our emergency funds and bought me a pair of black velvet shoes. Someone loaned me a pair of dainty rhinestone shoe clips. Someone else bought me a handkerchief embroidered all around with tiny silk roses. A pair of small pearl earrings with a matching choker appeared. Someone even found a long crinoline petticoat for me to wear.

On the eve of the coronation I said to Mama, "Wouldn't it be wonderful if Dad could be here?"

"He won't come," Mama said softly as she coaxed my hair into finger waves. "It's too far."

"No," she repeated, "he won't come. Don't look for him."

My step-dad came home with a stunning surprise. After a long day at the mill, he'd gone to Bemidji and purchased my first corsage! How proud he was as he pinned a cluster of baby roses to the left shoulder of the vanilla cream gown.

Even in the excitement I recognized what a sacrifice that must have been.

Then we packed ourselves into the cab of our old truck and away we went to the big event.

Lance Reed, my prince of the evening, offered my dress a compliment. I thought he might be lying but I told him he looked nice, too.

After the crowning of the seniors and a brief but pompous procession, I leaped from the stage and was running to get my coat when someone called my name. Looking up I saw Dad standing on the balcony!

He'd come through a storm to be with me for this not-so-special event that had been transformed to monumental proportions by the loving sacrifice of my family and the sincere concern of my relatives.

So the tattered gown became a testament to their deep—but generally unspoken and rarely demonstrated—care for that funny awkward girl from the poor side of the railroad tracks.

Dirty Indians

GEORGE ONE ROAD had been drinking for several days when he tumbled into a ditch full of cold water and fell on his face. Suddenly he was sober enough to acknowledge the empty ache in his belly and realize he hadn't eaten since the day before yesterday. Physically tormented by such prolonged hunger, he turned his reluctant feet toward home.

Night was pressing against the windows when Minnie put her embroidery aside, cupped her hand over the glass chimney of the kerosene lamp and blew it out.

Almost simultaneously she heard her husband fumbling at the door of their small house. She stepped to the middle of the room but ignored his clumsy efforts to get inside. When he finally flung the door open and stumbled into the sparse but cozy front room, she gave him a long, icy stare and turned her back on his painful remorse.

Once inside, George didn't feel so hungry anymore and he knew he couldn't ask Minnie for food now. He looked around the room and saw five-year-old Tillie asleep in the big chair. He saw Minnie's contempt, too. But he put a shoulder against her coldness and pushed his way back into their lives.

He forced his heavy feet to climb the narrow stairway to their attic bedroom. His face was already twisted into a grimace of self-loathing when he fell across the old chenille bedspread that covered the brass bed.

Tillie was awake now. Quietly she slipped from the chair and crept up the worn wooden steps behind her father. She covered him with her tattered doll blanket and curled up beside him. George smiled and turned to face her. Then he wrapped his arms around her warmth, kissed her pretty nose and fell into a peaceful sleep.

When Minnie heard her husband begin to snore she went up the stairs, too. As she gazed down on her dear ones, Tillie looked up and smiled.

Minnie spread a large warm quilt over her husband and child. Then with the light touch acquired over long years of experience, she picked his pockets while Tillie watched. She found a brass whistle, a small jack knife, a bottle opener, a few crumpled bills and a handful of coins. She put the coins in her pocket, rolled the paper money into a tight bundle and removed a large shiny knob from the bedstead head. Then she tucked the money inside, replaced the knob and went downstairs. Tillie slipped out of her father's arms and followed her mother into the small kitchen.

The pantry was located under the attic steps and when Minnie opened the pantry door, Tillie crept back into the dark depths. Moments later she emerged with a red and white baking powder can. Without rising to her feet Tillie removed the lid and mother stooped down to put the coins inside. Tillie replaced the lid and returned the can to its hiding place. Then they both went to sleep in Tillie's small bed.

In the morning, Minnie busied herself at the wood stove and soon the aroma of bacon and coffee wafted itself invitingly over the sleeping man. Slowly his eyes opened. He stretched, yawned and finger-combed his tousled hair.

He touched the quilt and smiled toward the rafters, grateful for his wife's consideration of his comfort. For a single moment he was happy. But his happiness turned to shame when he recalled his binge drunk. He didn't know how he could face his family again. Nevertheless, he got up and went down stairs.

Minnie had filled the chipped enamel basin with warm water and hung a fresh towel on a nail over the washstand. She had folded his clean clothes neatly and placed them on a kitchen chair. Like an obedient child he stripped, bathed and dressed.

When he was fit to sit at Minnie's table, she put a dish heaped with food at the head of the table and poured two cups of strong coffee. As George began to eat, Minnie picked up her cup and went to sit near the front window where Tillie sat on the floor quietly playing with her rag doll and the small tattered blanket.

Minnie didn't speak to her husband all that day. There was nothing she could say. There was nothing he could say. It had all been said before. Their silence fell around the child like ashes from a forgotten fire.

The next morning Minnie gave him some money and he took Tillie to the general store in the white man's village. Hand in hand they walked along. Together they watched bluebirds swoop through the bright sky and golden butterflies dance with windblown flowers.

At the store, Tillie carefully selected a few pieces of penny candy and a Bit-O-Honey bar. She got a Butterfinger for Mama, and George purchased a bag of Bull Durham cigarette tobacco. When he asked for a book of matches, the skinny proprietor scowled and handed it to him. But as George reached for it with trembling fingers, the proprietor laughed scornfully and let it fall on the counter between them.

George pulled himself into a military posture, picked up his book of matches and met the other man's staring blue eyes.

"Thank you, kind sir," he said with exaggerated tones of gratefulness. Then he brushed his thick hair back from his face in a manner that made the white man acutely aware of his own shiny almost-bald head, except for the long, blond comb-over.

George turned to leave. He and Tillie had already reached the door when the proprietor muttered a string of epithets that ended with "those dirty Indians."

Later they walked to the small public park and George pushed Tillie on the swing. The rusty scream of the old chain irritated the man but it thrilled the child. Higher and higher she flew until she felt the clouds touch her upturned face, then she closed her eyes and kissed the bottom of the sky.

When a group of loud, unwashed blond children arrived in ragged overalls, George took Tillie from the swing and they quickly left the park. But not before she'd heard one of the boys say, "Those dirty Indians should make their own park."

That's when George picked Tillie up, swung her over his head and set her on his shoulders. She felt very tall as she bobbed along and very proud of her strong father.

Later they stopped to watch a mallard hen and nine fluffy ducklings feed in the water-filled ditch near the dusty road. Tillie tried to coax them to her with a piece of candy.

George laughed softly, "Ducks don't eat candy, Baby. Next time we'll bring bread."

Tillie could already hear her mother's playful mocking complaint. "What! I wear myself out around here trying to keep us fed and you want to feed my good bread to a duck?"

Just then a car came along. Someone leaned from the window and shouted, "Get out of the road, you dirty Indians!"

George took Tillie's small hand and pulled her along until the car was out of sight. Then he waited patiently as she stopped to pick up a few pretty stones for Mama. She held them up for him to see but he was far away, lost in thought.

Minnie called him "Moody" when he pulled himself into his shell like this. Tillie knew they would linger here and there along the way for hours. She knew they would not reach home until the stars came out. She knew he would not speak and she was silent, too.

At last they reached home and when Minnie saw the helpless anger smoldering in her husband's troubled eyes, she prayed for one more sober day. Just one.

Then she prepared a meatless supper and they made happy chatter around their small table. Later she surprised her family with cookies and lemonade, an extravagance purchased with her secret coins.

That night Minnie washed Tillie's face, neck and ears. Tillie washed her own hands and feet. Then she put on her faded pink pajamas and George carried his sweet smelling baby up the stairs to her cot under the east window. He was in a good mood now so he told a story about a little girl and a blue butterfly. Then he tucked the blanket carefully around her.

When he leaned down to kiss her, Tillie wrapped her small arms around his neck and pulled his ear to her mouth.

"You're my big dirty daddy," she whispered, "and I'm your little dirty Indian girl."

There was a war inside of George that night. He didn't like to think of how it was going to end, so he went and found his brother, Richard.

Three days later he came home tired, hungry and unwashed.

Minnie waited as he fumbled at the door and wept as he disappeared up the attic steps. Then Tillie crept up the stairs to cover him with her small blanket.

The Yellow Dog

IT HAPPENED on the Leech Lake Reservation, not so long ago, that an Anishinabe family was returning to Oak Point after visiting relatives on the shores of Steamboat Lake.

They were riding in a weathered buckboard wagon pulled by two brown mares. In the wagon were the father, mother, their young son and the boy's big yellow dog. Although the dog belonged to the boy, the mother loved that dog so much that she had beaded a wide blue collar for him.

Of course, the dog was happy to have the collar. Everyone noticed that since receiving the fine gift he had become rather proud. He stepped high and walked tall.

Now as they went along the father said, "It's such a nice evening. I think we should pull up under the trees and camp out. We have enough food. We can get up early and reach home before dark."

The mother was delighted and soon the wagon was standing under a tree with the horses hobbled nearby. While the boy gathered wood, the mother spread blankets under the wagon. The father built a nice fire and the woman began cooking rice and dried fish. The boy found some nice green sorrel and wild onions to add to the meal and as they sat waiting for the soup to cook, the father began speaking of his boyhood.

He spoke for a long time and the family listened. The dog watched the man closely and the firelight danced in his dark eyes. When the woman told of her early life the dog seemed particularly interested. At last the boy spoke briefly about an otter he had seen swimming in the river that day.

Then the father had something more to say. Afterwards the woman spoke and then the boy. Before the father could open his mouth, the dog leaped up and shouted, "I have something to say!"

Everyone was surprised. They didn't know the dog could talk.

The boy clapped his hands with delight.

Mother laughed.

But the father picked up a stick of wood and hit the dog.

The dog yelped loudly and fled into the forest.

The boy began to cry.

The mother scowled.

The father shouted, "Quick! Put everything back into the wagon. I'll hitch up the horses. We've got to get out of here right now! There's a mocking spirit in this place and we cannot spend the night here!"

The mother and the boy did as the father said but they were not pleased.

They rode along in silence all the rest of the night. Then just as day began to peek through the trees, they pulled onto their road. Looking toward their small house they saw something sprawled in front of the door.

It was the big yellow dog!

When he saw his people he ran to them, barking and leaping. He wagged himself so hard that he almost twisted himself into a circle.

The boy jumped from the wagon and embraced the happy dog.

The mother stepped down from the wagon and patted the dog on the head.

Even the father was glad to see that the dog had returned home.

Everyone was happy but the dog never spoke again.

Some say it was the mocking spirit that gave the dog the ability to speak. Some say there was magic in the blue collar. Others believe it was the work of the Little People.

But it was clear to all that anger, fear and authority had forever silenced the wonderful talking dog.

The Scheming Son

IT HAPPENED that an infant boy's father was taken suddenly in a fatal car crash. In her grief and despair, his mother became overly protective of her child, and never required him to accept any responsibilities.

At first, the sympathetic people in the community had come with fish and meat to help the woman and her young son. Later, the elders advised her repeatedly: "You have brothers. They can show him how to hunt and catch fish. They can teach him to be responsible. They can raise him to be a good man."

But the boy would look at his mother with mournful eyes. His lips would quiver and he would run away. She would find him sulking and pacify him with promises. He would reward her with hugs and kisses and a beautiful smile.

Whenever the elders would persist in advising her to allow her male relatives to raise the boy to be responsible and provide for her she would respond sadly, "He doesn't want to hunt or fish and I want him to be happy."

After a while, the elders realized they could do nothing, and left the two alone.

The woman continued to work in their small garden alone, carrying water and wood without his help. She was strong enough for both of them, she thought, as she took the axe and the wedge into the forest to cut down a dry tree. Then she would limb it and drag it to the yard, where she would saw it and chop it into small enough pieces for the wood stoves. So she provided the wood to bake their bread and heat their winter house.

As the years passed, the boy became a man and his mother became tired working in the garden. She began to weaken under her burdens of work and worry, and dragged home smaller and smaller trees.

One day she asked her son to help her in the garden.

The surprise in his face quickly turned to anger. "You do it!" he shouted. "I'm not a woman!"

Hurt and shocked, she pleaded, "I'm no longer able to do such heavy work. You're strong. Why won't you help me?"

"Because I don't want to," he snapped.

"Well, I want you to," she said, raising her voice.

"If you don't leave me alone, I'll kill myself," he threatened.

He ran into the garage and pulled down a long rope. He pushed angrily past her as she tried to block his way. He walked quickly to a tall tree and climbed to a stout limb.

She begged him to come down.

Ignoring her, he tied one end of the rope around the limb and the other around his neck.

She watched in horror as he pushed himself off the limb and dropped toward the ground. She covered her eyes. A scream rose up out of her as she fell to her knees, afraid to look up.

Suddenly she heard an awful laugh. She opened her frightened eyes and saw her son standing under the tree, the long rope swinging in the wind.

Sick with shock and despair, the woman staggered into the house. Her son smirked as he coiled the rope and carried it to the garage.

A few weeks later, she asked him again for some assistance.

He stared at her for a long time. "Do you want me to die?" he said.

She shook her head helplessly and walked to the garden alone.

A month passed. The pain in her back forced her to ask him to gather a little wood for the stove. She lay on her bed with an arm across her eyes. She did not watch as he walked past her. She knew that he was going to get the rope. He paused at the doorway but she said nothing, so he left.

Minutes passed. Then a half hour. Then an hour. The son did not return. The woman got up to look for him, to see what he was doing.

"Has he gone for wood?" she wondered.

Under the tree she saw him. Her son was hanging, lifeless, from the stout limb. The toes of his shoes traced slow circles in the dust as the wind turned his heavy body.

After the three-day wake, the woman buried her son and went to live with her younger sister.

Several weeks later, a neighbor brought her a new rope to replace the one he'd borrowed. He told her that he'd needed a short rope. She had not been home at the time, so he'd gone into the garage and found the long rope. He'd cut off the few feet he'd needed and put the rope back where he'd found it, coiled on the high shelf.

Evening in Paris

G ERALDINE POURED a small amount of lilac-scented bubble bath into the swirling water as she filled the large porcelain tub. She fin-ger-combed her long hair, twisted it into two loose braids and tied them together on the top of her head. Slowly she undressed, allowing her clothes to fall to the floor in artful disarray. With a long sigh she lowered herself into the water and heaped piles of bubbles on her breasts and shoulders.

It was the early 1950s and cinema loomed large and glamorous in the cen-ter of her rather small and quiet world. Her daydreams were peopled with the photogenic characters that she'd seen again and again on what was grandly referred to as the silver screen.

She wondered if the alluring Jane Russell tied her raven tresses in a loose knot on the top of her head when she took long hot baths in her large and lovely Hollywood home. Raising one lean leg out of the water, she watched the bubbles run down her graceful ankle and along her nicely muscled calf. After sponging gently she reluctantly rose from the bubbles, and stepped from the tub. She dried her young body with tender hands and stared at herself in the mirror for a long time.

"Just think," she told her reflection, "it wasn't very long ago that you looked almost like a boy. Now look at yourself! Why, You're actually... pretty."

She slipped into her blue chenille robe, picked up her clothes and went down the hall to her room. The rosebud and butterfly wallpaper which she'd watched her father hang just six months before, was now covered with pictures of movie stars. She'd cut them carefully from magazines and, against her father's wishes, she'd taped them to the wall. She even had real autographed photographs of Esther Williams, Gary Cooper, June Allyson, Doris Day and Gene Kelly.

Geraldine didn't have a lot of money to spend on clothing so she selected everything with extreme care. Now she dressed in those well-chosen articles and was once again astonished at her recently developed beauty.

When she was clothed to perfection, she brushed her long lustrous hair and turned it around her fingers in a Lauren Bacall pageboy. Then she pulled on her white bobby socks and pushed her feet into her new shoes. Lastly she dabbed a touch of Evening in Paris under her ears, on her wrists and behind her knees.

Her beauty ritual completed, she opened the front door, took a deep breath, pulled back her shoulders, stepped off the porch and went to meet Carmen and Lucille.

They'd been best friends for less than a year. Except for going to work, they went everywhere together. They shared their secrets and their dreams, their sweaters and their nail polish and couldn't remember what their lives had been before they'd met.

Geraldine smiled as she thought of the two young women who had grown so close to her in such a short time. They were each so different. One tall. One short. One was quiet. One was loud. But they were like sisters now and she couldn't wait to see them.

She'd looked forward to Friday night all week long. It was the break she needed after working four ten-hour days at the Chef Café. It promised to be a great event, too. First the three friends planned to see a movie. Then they'd go Carmen's and listen to her collection of popular 78 rpm records on her portable phonograph.

She'd promised her mother that if it got too late she'd spend the night with Carmen and walk home in the morning.

Now she listened to the sharp click of the metal heel cleats striking the concrete as she walked along Franklin Avenue in her shiny brown penny loafers. Like most of her friends, she'd dropped out of school at sixteen. At seventeen, she still lived with her parents but she had a job now, and purchased her clothes, shoes, and perfume with her wages.

She walked the three long blocks to Fourth Avenue where she turned toward the Chateau Theater. A vagrant breeze lifted the hair from her shoulders and swept her skirt close around her hips. Her small red leather purse bumped against her thigh as she walked. Inside the purse was the money she'd made taking and filling orders for hungry customers, some of whom were gracious and courteous, some of whom were vulgar and disrespectful.

When she reached the theater she waited under the marquee for Carmen and Lucille. They would soon arrive from the opposite direction.

Geraldine tapped her foot as she waited. It was not a gesture of impatience but an opportunity to see how the new dimes in her shoes glinted under the marquee lights. All the young women put dimes in their loafers so they always had coins for a couple of phone calls if they should need assistance.

At last she saw them walking arm-in-arm. She hurried toward them, calling their names. Being thoroughly engaged in a bit of spicy gossip, they didn't even hear her. But when they saw her, they closed the distance between them with long, quick steps.

They shared the gossip with Geraldine as they joined the line that had formed before the ticket booth. Then they purchased their tickets, got some popcorn and entered the already darkened chamber of fantasy and dreams.

It was easy for Geraldine to accept the Hollywood magic of glamour and romance. She really believed that men like Clark Gable fell in love with women like Claudette Colbert, Barbara Stanwyck, Katherine Hepburn and Ingrid Bergman.

She felt as glamorous as a movie star when she copied their hairstyles, their gestures and their fine speech. She practiced Judy Garland dance steps and pinned her hair up like Betty Grable. Although she didn't smoke, she'd learned how to hold a cigarette like Lana Turner and could drink Coke like Bette Davis drank a dry martini.

But tonight the three young women wept through the tragic love of Van Johnson and Elizabeth Taylor. Later they linked arms as they walked down the street humming the haunting pathos of *The Last Time I Saw Paris*.

"It isn't fair!" Geraldine cried. "She was so young! So beautiful."

"Get a hold of yourself," Carmen advised. "It's just a movie. It's all tinsel and smoke and mirrors."

"But those kind of things do happen," Lucille said. "Life can be unkind and unfair."

"Unfair," grieved Geraldine. "Unkind."

Then they hummed the music again as they entered the deserted Franklin Steele Square recreation area. Carmen and Geraldine danced cheek-to-cheek through the dark park. Then Lucille cut in and Geraldine danced alone.

With her blue skirt floating around her she lamented, "Oh, Fred Astaire! Where are you when I need you?"

When they arrived at the run-down building where Carmen shared a second floor flat with her mother, Geraldine maneuvered the stairs without missing a beat. A few Rita Hayworth steps between the landings made her ascent a stunning achievement.

"Going down will be even better," she promised. "I'll do my Ann Miller routine." Then she added with an exaggerated sigh, "Wouldn't it be wonderful if Gene Kelly were waiting under the street lamp tonight?"

Carmen and Lucille tried to imagine which handsome leading man they'd like to meet under the corner street light.

Then Carmen popped a bowl of popcorn, drizzled it with melted butter and gave it a quick sprinkle of salt. Lucille rolled up the tattered rugs and Geraldine selected records from Carmen's outstanding collection of music and songs. Her mother had begun the collection during the big band era and had passed it on to Carmen on her sixteenth birthday.

They danced for hours, so it was pretty late when Geraldine decided to walk home alone. Although Carmen and Lucille protested, Geraldine leaned against the door and extended a limp hand in a tragic gesture of farewell. Then she brushed the back of her long fingers languidly over her hair and said in a sultry voice, "Now is the hour when we must say goodbye."

"You should stay," urged Carmen.

"Don't worry," Geraldine told them, "it's not so far."

She was half way home when someone hit her on the head with a brick and dragged her behind the bushes under a large billboard. She was still struggling when her assailant punched her in the face several times. At last, she lay still and helpless.

When she regained consciousness it was daybreak. Her hair was caked with dried blood; her clothes were stained with grass and mud; her face was lacerated in several places; her watch and her purse were gone. She found her shoes, put them on and stumbled toward home. Because of the head injury, she staggered as she went along.

A car passed and a man shouted, "Hey! You drunken squaw! Get off the street! You're a disgrace to the neighborhood!"

At last she stood reeling in front of her parent's home. Because the key had been taken with her purse, she knocked softly and prayed her father would not be awakened.

She held her breath as the curtain was pulled aside. But it was her mother's tired face that peered out at her.

At first she didn't recognize her bloody daughter. When she did, she covered her mouth with both hands to stifle a scream.

For a moment she was paralyzed by shock and fear, then she pulled the door open and Geraldine fell into her arms.

"Mama," she moaned. "Oh, Mama."

Together they stumbled to the bathroom and Mama turned on the water. With gentle hands she helped Geraldine undress.

"Oh, my baby. My baby," she crooned, as she eased her battered child into the warm water.

After a thoughtful moment she asked, "What will I tell your father?"

"Tell him nothing," Geraldine whispered. "What can he do?"

"But your face..."

"Tell him I was dancing down Carmen's stairs and I fell. He'll believe that."

Mama wept quietly as she poured warm water over her darling's hair and tenderly washed mud from the bloody cuts.

"Who would do such a thing?" she wondered out loud.

It wasn't Gene Kelly.

Field of Many Dreams

SHE CAME EARLY, before dawn. I heard her raspy breath before she tapped her arrival signal on my old blue door. Quickly I arose, pushed my feet into my waiting slippers, pulled on my fuzzy robe and hurried to let her in. I would have fallen into her arms but there was no room for me. Close to her bony chest she clutched a pillowcase bulging with unknown contents.

"Come," she whispered. "We must hurry to the field of many dreams. I have food for the journey." But I was reluctant.

"Surely such a journey would be difficult for this old one," I sighed. "Certainly too far for me who grows breathless on the stoop after three short steps. Really it is impossible. I cannot go."

But she would not listen.

"Bring a blanket," she demanded and turned abruptly.

I could not allow her to make such a dangerous journey alone so I picked up my blanket and followed her out into the darkness. As I stumbled after her she began to sing a little song. After I'd heard the words several times I joined my voice with hers and our combined volume seemed to stir the leaves of nearby trees.

"We are coming! We are coming! Open the gate for us. We are welcome. We are welcome. Welcome in the field of many dreams."

Soon we were marching in unison and my tiredness drained away. My steps were light. My legs were strong. I could walk on forever!

The sky was filled with a rosy glow and two huge blue ponies waited patiently on top of the hill. But as we crested they ran from us and joined a distant herd where they melted into a fiery sunrise.

"There," she said at last, "there is our field of many dreams."

Looking down the hill I saw a small dark lake surrounded by a thousand white daisies shining like stars in the grassy field still caught in the shadow of the hills around us. It was entirely enclosed by a willow fence and kept inviolate by a sturdy gate. With uncommon grace she leaned forward into a splendid curtsy and the gate opened. We entered like thieves cloaked in shadows. We hardly dared to breathe. We were as silent as the mice that scurried from our furtive feet.

I was going to close the gate behind us but she stopped me with a gesture. We walked closer to the water and I spread the blanket on the ground. She put down the pillowcase and began removing the contents. There was bread, liverwurst, pickles, oranges, a jar of sweetened tea, two knives and mother's flower vase.

I took the vase to the lake and filled it with cool water. Then I began picking daises until a beautiful bouquet looked up at me with stunned and golden eyes. I looked up, too. The sky brightened overhead. Soon this field would become a large fragrant bowl filled with the light and songs of morning.

I returned to the blanket. She opened her hands to receive the gift of flowers. Then I sat down on my knees beside her, we faced the rising sun and waited. Suddenly we were drenched in a great spray of dawn.

I watched as her gray hair darkened. She grew young and beautiful before me. Then I raised my youthful hands and with quick deft fingers I explored the soft rose petal skin of my face. I pulled my braid forward and saw that my hair had grown thick and dark.

It was always like this in the field of many dreams.

After we ate, we danced. After we danced, we sang. After we sang, we slept.

While we slept, we dreamed. After we dreamed, we ate again.

At last the sun moved on and left us in shadows. We were leaving the dream field, changing back to our former selves. It all had happened in an instant.

We returned everything to the pillowcase. My sister began walking up the hill and I followed with the folded blanket.

We stepped through the gate. Slowly she closed it. Then we turned and walked away. Our feet were heavy. We were not strong. Our breath was labored and our faces creased with the joys and hardships of many winters.

While each step carried us farther from the field of many dreams and closer to the place we lived, my memory of the experience diminished.

Leaving me at my old blue door she held my hands as I stared out at her.

"It's all right to forget because we can go again tomorrow," she promised.

Wanabozho Returns

ONE DAY the elected tribal officials were having a meeting at the tribal headquarters in Cass Lake. They had met to talk about reservation problems and seek solutions. But because of deficient funds and a per diem squabble, they were making no progress.

So, one of the elected men went for a walk along the lake. While he was walking, he was thinking. Then a strange thing happened. He met Wanabozho.

At first he couldn't believe what he saw. But Wanabozho stood before the man and said, "My son, you look troubled."

The man said, "Yes, I am troubled. The people have lost confidence in the Reservation Business Committee and the Executive Counsel of the Minnesota Chippewa Tribe. Yet we really are trying to determine what will be best for all the people. There are only a few good jobs. So many of our people do not live well. Fathers are discouraged. Many leave their families. Mothers are discouraged. Some will not care for their children. Many children are quite unhappy. It is a poor time for budget cuts."

"Yes," Wanabozho replied. "I have seen the human pain in this community. I too am troubled by so much sorrow. I am also puzzled, for I remember when there was enough good work for everyone to do. The people lived well.

Parents were proud to provide for their families and care for their children. Children honored their parents and were happy."

"Ah," the elected man sighed. "We hope to restore such domestic tranquility. We have established numerous programs to overcome the despair that is rampant on this reservation."

Wanabozho went on speaking. "There were many deer. Enough for all. Enough to share. The sinew made strong thread. The hides were rubbed with brains to make them soft. They were smoked over a slow fire. They made fine garments. It was good and pleasant work. The meat was cut, sliced thin and chopped fine. It was mixed with herbs and vegetables to make good meals. Nothing was wasted, nothing was scorned."

The elected man explained that the reservation had a food distribution program and Social Services could provide clothing vouchers. He assured Wanabozho that the people would have what they needed.

But Wanabozho did not seem to be listening.

He took something from his pocket. He showed the man that he had one dollar in coins. He laid the money on a rock and continued to speak. "Long ago the people lived as they would. They lived with the land and they lived with the times. Now we see that many things have changed. Brother deer is bought and sold. Our children have become merchandise. And greed receives honor."

The elected man raised his voice. "You will find that compromise is often essential."

"Even in this time, with confusion everywhere, I understand this much," Wanabozho said. "The people cannot return to our old ways and you cannot lead as our elders led. Tell the people they must make a place for themselves in this new time."

The man was encouraged. He felt that he had found some answers. He was excited and eager to return to the meeting.

He put out his hand toward Wanabozho, but Wanabozho stepped back and turned his face away.

Wanabozho spoke once more. "Tell me, my son, why have you continued to overlook the exploitation of my children? Why do you reward courtesy with contempt? How do you justify the oppression of your sisters and brothers? How do you explain the institution of nepotism in a way that those excluded from benefits can appreciate? Why do you skim government money and casino profits for yourself?"

Suddenly the man was alone. He thought, "Perhaps I have been dreaming." But when he turned to leave, he saw the coins shining in the sun.

When he returned to the meeting he said nothing, for he was ashamed.

Hometown Street

A CHILD IS A GIFT expected for several months before he arrives. The delivery usually takes place at dawn, just as the rising sun tinges the day with rose.

After weeks of preparation and hours of travail, the infant lies in his mother's waiting arms. No mother can forget that first embrace. Even elder women will tell you, "I still remember how he felt in my arms when I held him for the first time."

A mother will hover over the sleeping infant and gaze at her dearest one for hours. The child will remember how her breath covered his upturned face. She will do all she can to protect her darling from whatever threats may be waiting in their future. She will not hesitate to challenge an angry wild bear or a mindless system, in defense of that child.

When illness strikes, she will rush him to a healer for help and pray fervently for the little one's recovery. She will hold the child close to her breast and be his shield against every woe and every foe. She will nurture that tiny life with good food, constant care and a daily dose of her patient, loyal love. Her child will be safe, she promises.

Of course, the toddler will have frequent falls, but she will be there to kiss away the pain. With bandages and salve she will mend the scrapes and scratches.

At last she surrenders him to the care of the public school system. This separation can be painful, especially if the appearance of the child is unusual in any way. The mother hopes the child will be accepted, but fears that he will be ridiculed and humiliated daily. She vows to be his tree of life and his comfort through every storm.

"Oh, Mama," he begs, confirming her fears. "Let me stay home with you. Please, don't make me go to school. Nobody likes me. I have no friends. I want to stay home with you. Please!" She holds him close and weeps into his hair.

But state law demands that the child fulfill an education requirement and the mother sees no alternative. She tries to make the most of what is an ordeal for both of them. Her love will see him through, she pledges. She will be his unfailing champion.

But as the child matures, he spends more time away from her and she doesn't know what he is forced to endure. She suspects that it is too terrible to hear, but she wants to know. He learns to protect her by hiding the truth about what he faces every day.

He doesn't tell her about the terrible teasing and the cruel conduct of other children. He doesn't tell her that he is even ridiculed by adults, who should know better. He doesn't mention how many times he is forced to endure injustices because attractive children receive more positive attention from certain schoolteachers and other staff.

He might say, "I like you, Mom. Because you always try to be fair."

Finally he leaves school behind and picks up wisps of old dreams that came unraveled over the long tormented years. He finds them scattered like neglected gifts, but he gathers them up and from this is begins building a life for himself.

Somewhere on his journey his vision begins to fail, just as doctors had predicted. He does what he can to prepare for the blindness that will follow. He continues to find fulfillment in his woodwork, stone carving and his dogs. He also enjoys the reputation of one who makes good, sweet wine that he shares with family and friends. He is kind and generous toward his mother for he remembers her long grief. His brothers and sisters respect the man he has become. His nieces and nephews adore him. He has some loyal lifelong friends. So it's a good life and he accepts it as a gift. But the ridicule, harassment and abuse go on in the community he calls home, and late one winter night it comes to a violent end.

Nearly every night he walks alone with his dogs. Knowing how dangerous the hometown streets have become for him, his sister begs him to stay home and be safe. But he refuses. He believes he has a right to walk the public streets of his hometown. It is, he tells her, his own God-given right.

"What God has given, no one can take," he says. "Don't worry, Sis. I know the streets, like I know your hand."

But on a dark November night, he is accosted and assaulted by four young men, under the influence of alcohol and other mind-altering chemicals.

Many local residents believe persons who provide drugs and alcohol to minors must be held accountable, and have petitioned the hometown authorities to take action. But nothing has been done.

The intoxicated teenagers are enraged by the blind man's insistence that they will not force him from a public street. Surely they demand his money as well. He is alone and far from the shelter of his mother's arms. He is keenly aware of the distance and the years that separate him from her first embrace.

They follow him down Second Street with threats and taunts. He finds no safe place on that hometown street and becomes increasingly frightened. Five witnesses see the brutal attack. They hurry to their respective homes, lock themselves inside and call 911.

Someone said a cop had been there five minutes before the attack, but he is gone now.

Afterwards, law enforcement personnel from four agencies arrive to watch him die on the hometown street, his blood freezing on the concrete.

They would not see the angel at his side and would not know how his mother's warm breath fell over his cold, pale face.

His dog would carry a bloody glove home to his waiting mother. "He was trying to tell me that my son needed me. The dog wanted me to know that my son was in trouble. Just then the police came and told me they had found him. They said he was dead!"

Preparations are made for his final rest.

At the wake his nieces and nephews draw pictures of his dogs and place the love gifts in the wooden casket so he'll see them when he opens his eyes on the other side.

After the funeral, a candlelight vigil is held at the place of death. There the wistful voice of a child is overheard saying, "He was the best uncle a girl ever had."

They say several youth want to organize a volunteer foot patrol so other people will be safe on their hometown street. They say the family of the murdered man will hold an annual candlelight vigil on the hometown street as a memorial to the gift he was and shall forever be.

So a son, a brother, an uncle and friend is laid to rest and some residents try to remember the last time they felt safe on their hometown streets. They wonder if this senseless murder and this lonely death will be the impetus needed to carry residents away from their fear, denial, impotence and apathy. They wonder if a community of courage can rise from the bloody concrete of a hometown street.

eAmik ('Beaver)

THE TIME HAD COME.
He would leave the colony, his family and his friends. He would venture downriver to establish his own home. Eventually he would have new friends and a family of his own.

He knew it would be dangerous. But he was prepared to confront all natural enemies, all four-legged predators.

He would be industrious and cautious. Like all his kind, he would do what had to be done and he would do it well.

He savored the care and concern of the community. He was a product of the watchful elders, the compassionate members of his extended family. Now he sensed that he might not see his parents, siblings, aunts or uncles again.

They said their goodbyes all around, and he hurried away with an unnamed ache in his brave wild breast. But he was also aware of a new excitement, the thrill of independence and an opportunity to measure himself against his world. He was eager to find his place in the great web of life.

He made his way slowly down the winding river and many miles later found a promising habitat, complete with an abandoned lodge. Here the river was shallow but he had superb dam-building skills. The old lodge was in disrepair but he was confident that he could bring it up to standard.

He turned his attention to locating a dam site. He did this without difficulty, as the river ran through a narrow channel under a road. In this place the water would be easily controlled. He recognized the potential of the greatest compensation for the least amount of effort.

He would work at night when the "road beast" passed less frequently. Quickly he cut sticks and poles to form the framework. He packed the frame with mud and roots. He tumbled large stones along the bottom of the river to add strength to the structure.

One day it stood complete! He was great with pride. He thought of his father and decided he would visit the colony of his youth while he waited for the water to rise around the lodge.

His mother was anxious that day and sensed his return. At last she went down the river to meet him. When they saw each other, they chuckled with delight and hurried into a loving embrace. They bumped noses frequently as they swam back to the colony.

What a glad reunion! There was much nose bumping and grooming in the happy lodge. This demonstration of deep affection meant so much to him that he was tempted to remain with the colony.

But in the end he thought of his own lodge. He wanted to see how much water the dam had held. So he began his solo journey.

When he reached his lodge, he was dismayed to hear water running over the dam.

Quickly he inspected the damage and wondered what had happened. There was a strange and awful odor all around the dam area. He did not know it, but beaver persecutors had destroyed his wonderful dam and launched a relentless campaign to discourage the beaver from living there.

But now he thought perhaps he'd built a poorly designed dam, so he modified the plan and began building anew.

When he finished the new dam he added a small trough at the top. Now some of the water would be allowed to spill over and he could still control the flow to maintain a desirable water level for his home.

When the beautiful dam had been in place for about two weeks, the vandals returned. Soon they had destroyed the second dam.

Again he built a dam. This time he built it well inside the culvert. Almost fiercely, he closed the flow completely.

After several attempts, the persecutors succeeded in destroying the new dam, too. Then they installed a foolish-looking iron gate at one end of the culvert.

Once more he brought building materials and entered at the unguarded end of the culvert. Yes, he built the dam again and it was very strong.

He had never thought of death and did not know that the persecutors, being unable to outwit him, would now seek a means to kill him.

So they laid a trap in one of his work canals. He saw and avoided it. Not because he was fearful, but because strange objects are best left alone.

Six dams would be destroyed and the lodge plundered repeatedly. Yes, he was discouraged. No, he would not be driven away. This was his home.

But late one night, too weary for caution, he was caught in the trap. That ugly, awkward, clumsy, murdering metal contraption devised by the two-leggeds for persecution and death, for profit, greed and convenience.

The trap held him under water as he struggled mightily for his life. He died by inches, full of fear and agony. The images of his anxious mother, proud father and fond sisters passed before his eyes.

No trapper came to claim his hide. No tobacco was sprinkled over him with an honoring prayer. Death was his only witness, bloody ragged death. Naked, raw and ugly death.

Two wandering dogs found his body. They tore him to pieces and fought for the tender portions. They snarled over his fine tail.

Our Anishinabe-Ojibwe people believe that only the most foolish of two-leggeds would allow dogs to eat beaver flesh. For there was a time in the long, long ago that Beaver was very great. But that is another story.

About the Author

A NNE M. DUNN (b. 1940) is an Anishinabeg-Ojibwe grandmother story-teller. She was born on the Red Lake Reservation in northern Minnesota, was enrolled at the White Earth Reservation, grew up on the Leech Lake Reservation and currently resides in Deer Lake, MN. Her books of stories include *When Beaver Was Very Great, Grandmother's Gift* and *Winter Thunder*.

As a young girl, she received many gifts from the wonderful storehouse of oral legends and animal fables of the Ojibwe, especially from her mother, Maefred Vanos Arey, and her grandmother, Frances Vanoss. Like many Native American children, Anne experienced life on reservation land and also lived for a time in Minneapolis. Anne grew up to become a licensed practical nurse, a mother of six, a newspaper reporter, and a professional storyteller.

About the Artist

A NNIE HUMPHREY is the daughter of Anne Dunn. She was born and raised in Cass Lake, MN on the Leech Lake Reservation. Annie served in the United States Marine Corps from 1990-1994. At the end of her service she was honorably discharged and then studied art at UND. Annie is a singer/songwriter as well as a visual artist. *Fire in the Village* is the second book of Anne Dunn's that she has illustrated. In December, 2015 she released *Uncombed Hair*, a CD available at cdbaby.com.